The Magic Of The Mountains

by

Mary-Beth Williams

Dales Large Print Books
Long Preston, North Yorkshire,
BD23 4ND, England.

British Library Cataloguing in Publication Data.

Williams, Mary-Beth
  The magic of the mountains.

  A catalogue record of this book is
  available from the British Library

  ISBN 1-84262-023-1 pbk

First published in Great Britain by Robert Hale Ltd., 1979

Published in Large Print 2000 by arrangement with
Robert Hale Ltd.

Dales Large Print is an imprint of Library Magna Books Ltd.

Printed and bound in Great Britain by
T.J. (International) Ltd., Cornwall, PL28 8RW

THE MAGIC OF THE MOUNTAINS

The world came to an end for Claire Matthews when her husband was killed on their wedding night. But her spirit kept her from going under and she decided to take a touring holiday. There she met Robert Hirst, also suffering from a lost love, and as they climbed the mountains together they began to find consolation. Married, and living in Switzerland, they climbed higher and higher peaks. But it was harder work to bring their fears, joys and mistakes to a happy resolution.

THE MAGIC OF THE MOUNTAINS

The world came to an end for Claire Matthews when her husband was killed on their wedding night. But her spirit kept her from going under and she decided to take a touring holiday. There she met Robert Hurst, also suffering from a lost love, and as they climbed the mountains together they began to find consolation. Married, and living in Switzerland, they climbed higher and higher peaks. But it was harder work to bring their fears, joys and mistakes to a happy resolution.

ONE

Anyone opening the door on that June evening would see what they imagined to be a schoolgirl sitting in the deep window embrasure of the sitting room, a schoolgirl with long dark hair loose about her shoulders and with arms and knees tented to make a secret place of her lap, where, possibly, her homework books lay under scrutiny. But if there was someone to approach, then the face upturned in surprise would be that of a young woman, whose violet eyes, caught unawares, would hold the pain that came less frequently, now, to haunt the gaze, but had still not quite gone away. There were no homework books on the young woman's lap but a newspaper, neatly folded at the crossword page. She idly tapped a blue ballpoint pen against her teeth as she sought the clue of twenty-one across: 'This lady likes a French pastry.'

She filled in her own name quite automatically, Claire. An anagram of éclair, of course, for she was familiar with the crossword compiler's style after many years of sharing the pastime with her father.

Five minutes later the whole crossword was completed and she looked out into the garden backing on to woodland where only the tallest trees were burnished by the setting sun.

'Now I have no more excuses not to finish my packing,' she decided, and uncurled almost unwillingly and stood up. 'I either have to call the whole thing off or get on with it.'

She watched heaven withdraw its golden light from the earth as though waiting for a sign, but now knew there would be no signs. No stars directing 'Come this way, Claire,' or voices of thunder roaring 'Don't do that, Claire'. She had waited for such things to happen after the first of the shock of Pete's death, but bereavement was such a personal thing that it dawned on her that nobody could experience it with one; they tried, with words, with gentle letters of condolence, but she felt like one trapped in some evil fairy ring where none other may enter and she couldn't get out.

It only seemed like eternity, however, the first weeks of the six months which had elapsed, and she had been out of the fairy ring for a long time, now; back to her job and the embarrassed silences of her colleagues followed by a kind of forced gaiety for her benefit. She was out of the wallowing and into a kind of twilight zone, where she acted her part of Ward Sister on Men's Surgical at St Columba's and then came home to the cottage she and Pete had bought to live in as man and wife; she having contributed the greater share because actually she earned rather more than Pete, and spent considerably less; and here she slid off her Nurse's cloak and became a frightened and lonely girl, looking for somewhere to turn, some guiding light to urge her on and, not finding either, tried to take up with the past, which is why she did the crosswords she and her father had faithfully shared together every Saturday evening at the Old Parsonage in days gone by, and why she read Cranford, again, and took her paints and easel into the woods to sketch trees, just two of her teenage occupations, recaptured without the joy of the first careless rapture.

Then a month ago she had looked at herself in the cheval mirror which she had bought at a sale and which Pete had said was spotty. She had not even taken her dark-blue overall off and her hair was escaping from the pins which held it in a fold at the back of her head. She examined her reflection with the same interest with which she regarded her patients and almost choked.

'My God, but you're sick, Claire! He wouldn't love you now. You look as insubstantial as Marley's ghost. You're a mess. You've stopped caring what people think. And they *must* be thinking. Those men on the ward deserve better than this!' and she waved a hand at her image. 'So what are you going to do about it, eh? There's a world out there. There's the future–' she winced as she said this. Had she secretly hoped there would be no future? That if she willed she could quickly obliterate herself? No, her father's teaching wouldn't allow the death of the spirit. The spirit was that spark which caused the phoenix to rise again. Nothing could kill the spirit. She made herself look forward and decided the first thing was to leave St Columba's and strike out in a new place where she was unknown. After the period of her notice she would take a holiday and then sell the cottage, cut loose, allow her spirit free rein and see where all this would lead her. She felt better for having reached these conclusions; not happy but better. She was brighter and more glowing on the wards, so that the men began to look at her with eyes in which the male animal stirred and wondered at the change in her.

The holiday was more difficult to plan. She didn't feel up to making the decisions about what to do with herself every day for a fortnight, and solved this by letting a package holiday firm decide for her. She bought a ticket for a coach tour round Britain. All she insisted on was a single room at the hotels where the party would stay each night. Even though some other lonely soul should share her seat in the coach, she couldn't bear to share with anyone else those moments before sleeping. Perhaps she still sub-consciously needed time to wallow and was leaving a vacant compartment in those days just in case.

Tomorrow she was to pick up the coach, with probably thirty or so other souls, at Victoria Coach Station, and the local train would take her in to Marylebone and launch her off on her adventure, or misadventure as it may well turn out to be.

'There's still time—' she panicked, as she bolted the front door. 'Do I really want to ride in a 'bus all round Britain? Why couldn't I have gone to Majorca or Capri?'

She went upstairs, regarded her suitcase lying open on the bed and then looked again at herself in the spotted cheval mirror.

'You're going, so get on with it,' she told her reflection curtly. 'It doesn't matter whether you go on a 'bus or in Concorde, you're making a break. Right?'

When the mirror didn't answer back she finished her packing and stood the case and a holdall together near the door, then she showered, donned her dainty nightdress of broderie anglaise, for the evening was warm, and, sitting on the side of the bed regarded Pete's one-sided smile in the photograph regarding her on the bedside table.

'Well, darling,' she said, 'I think I've at last accepted the fact that you're gone forever. This hasn't all been a nightmare and I must wake up once and for all. I know, if there *is* an after life, that you're probably busily living it, and that if you are allowed to think about me you'll be relieved that I'm coming to my senses. I also realize, had the boot been on the other foot, that you'd have got over me far quicker than I've got over you. I even sometimes think, though it hurts my pride to admit it, that I probably loved you best. You didn't want to rush into marriage, did you? Not until you'd got your Membership and a decent job. But with the cottage coming on to the market, so lovely and so – so commutable from St Columba's, maybe I did urge you on more than a little. I said I would buy it and live in it, anyway, and – bless you! – you said why didn't we get married and do without a honeymoon until we could afford one? We never did have that, did we, the honey-moon? And though I have your ring on my finger, and bear your name, we were never really married, were we, my darling? When a girl loses her husband on their wedding night there hasn't been an awful lot to make her feel any different, though she is still capable of feeling shocked and hurt and – and saddened beyond bearing. But lately, love, I've started to forget you a little. Oh! I remember the fun, and the parties, and the way you drove like a damned maniac in that damned car–! But I can't remember how it felt when we were together, the – the intimacy of our acquaintance. I suppose strong feelings have to be temporary or we could love, laugh or grieve ourselves to death. They say time heals all. Well, I'm not healed, yet, but I think I'm just turning the corner and I've made a sort of resolution not to keep looking back. I'm going on a coach tour tomorrow. Can you imagine me on a 'bus bumping all round the country? I think I shall laugh about that, eventually, and I haven't laughed in a long time. I haven't even read the itinerary properly, yet, because the only thing which seemed important when I booked was that the scenery should change before my eyes while I just sat tight and let it. I may even surprise myself by discovering Britain, and feel like a Roman legionnaire. After all, I have never been north of Oxford in my life, though I'm quite well acquainted with the Continent. So I'll say goodnight, now, darling, and settle down. It's only ten o'clock but I've got to get the eight-fifteen to Marylebone in the morning and I haven't been sleeping very well. Doctor Dickson gave me some mogodons but I flushed them away. I thought you'd like to know that because you were always against drugs being used as placebos, weren't you? So now, goodnight, and I'll see you when I get back in a fortnight and – if you can – wish me luck.'

Claire was amazed how well she had slept when the alarm buzzed at seven next morning. When she remembered what she was planning to do today her stomach produced 'butterflies', though this was not for the planned holiday, as such, but that she was at last doing something quite positive on her own.

It looked like being another warm, sunny day; June was literally flaming this year, and May had been lovely, weatherwise, too, with the darling buds tossing in what her grandmother had always called the 'May 'quake', a wind which was supposed to loosen all the roots and prepare the soil for a bumper harvest, and then opening into a show of blossom which had been quite breathtakingly beautiful.

She was at Victoria Coach Station quite early, looking at the luxury coach she would soon be occupying and hiding behind a cardboard cup of terrible tea as she watched her fellow passengers arriving, mostly noisily, and clambering into the interior. She saw a young woman, who was saying 'Call me Christine. I'm your courier', earnestly directing the coach-driver to stow away the luggage.

Two elderly women arrived, one tall and guardsmanlike and the other plump and motherly.

'So nice to have a companion, I think,' the

former announced. 'I didn't know whether I should risk it on my own. But now I've found you.'

'Mrs Font?' asked Christine.

'That's me,' said the female guardsman, to Claire's surprise. 'I haven't had a holiday since my husband died three years ago, but Miss Durrant says she'll look after me. Come on, dear!'

Claire smiled as the two women climbed into the coach. She thought she had better break cover and walked forward.

'My name is Matthews,' she told the courier.

'*Mrs* Matthews?' Christine glanced at her list and looked a little put out for a moment. Claire had clearly put her status on her application as widow, and obviously the courier hadn't expected to see a girl younger than herself. 'You're in seat twenty-six, Mrs Matthews. You have it all to yourself.'

'Thank you.' Claire got into the coach smiling politely where people were obviously regarding her, but without familiarity.

16

Not yet. She felt she had done enough for one day without rushing into friendships. She was even glad she had a double seat to herself. She was also glad Mrs Font and Miss Durrant had found each other as she would have resented being pushed into the company of another loner at first.

She had settled herself, still amazed by a certain grotesqueness in her choice of a holiday, when Alf and Rosie, Joe and Daisy arrived obviously more than full of holiday spirit already.

'Now Mr Twill,' Christine was saying, 'you're not on one of my tours again, are you? I had quite enough of you last year when we did the Lake District.'

Alf said something which had all five in roars of laughter. It was obvious that the life and soul of the party had arrived with these jovial East Enders.

'Cor!' said Alf, surveying the other occupants of the coach. 'We've arrived at a ruddy funeral or somefink. Look, Rosie, me old duch, we'll 'ave to get workin' on this lot

17

an' no mistake.'

'Go and sit down, ladies and gentlemen,' Christine said mock severely. 'Stop making nuisances of yourselves.'

Alf looked down at the top of Claire's head until her eyes were magnetized upwards.

'Cor!' he decided. 'Wot a little darlin'! I'm sittin' 'ere,' and down he plomped beside her.

Rosie, his wife, said a little nervously, 'Aw, come on, Alf. We're over 'ere. Stop muckin' abaht.'

'Muckin' abaht?' echoed Alf, and turned back to leer at Claire. 'Charnst would be a fine fing, eh, darlin'?'

Claire said softly, 'You're on my knitting, you know.'

Alf shot up and then grinned. ''Aving me on, are yer, beautiful? Where is 'e, eh? Your boy friend?'

'Alf!' protested Rosie.

'Come on, mate,' said Joe, quietly. 'Sit down with your old woman, or mine. I'm broadminded.'

All four laughed again and Christine was suddenly there, saying just the right thing and just enough.

'You must excuse this lot, Mrs Matthews, but they're ready for a holiday after working at Billingsgate all year. They're really quite harmless.'

'I'm sure,' Claire said with a quick smile across the aisle at her fellow travellers, who had got around to sorting out numerous carrier bags they had brought with them.

'What's this, Dais?' asked Rosie. 'What we want sandwiches for, eh? We stop for a you-know-what every two hours and can pick anything we like up then.'

'I'm only 'ere for the beer,' Alf told the coach. 'Keep your sandwiches.'

Claire was just thinking it was going to seem a very long fortnight when there was a distraction. The driver had climbed into his cab and it looked as though their departure was imminent when Christine began arguing with somebody on the steps of the coach.

'Yes, your ticket's valid, Doctor Hirst, but you're not on my list.'

'Then put me on,' came a masculine voice, sharply.

'I don't know that I can. It's easy for the office to hand out tickets at the last minute but not so easy for me to arrange accommodation.'

'Then I'll arrange it myself. Please don't concern yourself.'

The man, very hirsute with thick fair hair, a beard and moustache thrust down the aisle using a holdall as a battering ram. Alf ducked back into his seat as the man hesitated, and Claire tingled feeling her privacy was to be invaded yet again, but after the merest ricochet of glances he pressed on, stowed his bag in the rack, peeled a haversack from his shoulders and sat down in the middle of the back seat.

'A doctor!' Rosie said audibly. 'So if you get one of your spells, Alf, you'll be orlright.'

''Ave one of me spells on 'oliday, ducks? You're jokin'. I'm goin' to enjoy myself.

Good! We're off! Open the bar, Joe, an' 'and me a beer.'

Claire was glad when the coach was moving because everybody was busy looking out of the glare-proofed windows at the passing scene. Not that the passing scene was anything to boast about at first because it was mostly the M4 motorway and just like any other motorway. Claire had at last got around to studying the itinerary and discovered that they were to lunch at a hotel in Exeter, meander down to Land's End in time for tea and then spend the night at Ilfracombe, in North Devon.

Christine's voice droned into a microphone at intervals, but it was not a good mike and probably the Courier's natural voice would have given better service. It was rather like being on a station platform and not quite sure whether that was one's train the announcer had spoken of, or not, which was calling at OO-ham, and Brr-borough, Hoot-lington and Hum-bridge.

'If 'e, the doc, don't fancy yer, darlin', yer

can still count on me,' Alf broke into her thoughts to reassure her at one point. Claire's smile was wintry for such a warm day and the fish porter subsided.

Christine asked if she might join Claire at a table for two at lunch-time.

'Please do,' agreed the other.

'I'm not supposed to eat with guests, really. We have our own facilities laid on. But I wanted to apologize for the cockneys. They mean no harm.'

'No need to apologize for them,' Claire said. 'I haven't hired the 'bus to be exclusive.'

'Oh, well, that's OK. I thought, perhaps, you know?'

Claire didn't know and smiled encouragingly.

'I thought maybe your husband couldn't have been gone very long and that they might be annoying you.' Christine blushed.

'Some time now, actually,' Claire said, 'and he would have given Alf as good as he took. My husband was very sociable.'

She asked, under her breath, to be forgiven, knowing full well that though Pete was the life and soul of any party of his own cronies he would by now have blacked both Alf's eyes. He had been a strong, middle-weight amateur boxer.

'They can grow on you, people like Alf,' Christine went on. 'I had them last year and there were a couple from Beaconsfield on the tour, retired, refined and taking their first coach tour ever. Alf started on them the first day, backed up by Joe, who's quite amusing, too, in his own way. They called them Bert and Min, and by the third day these two were responding. At the finish they were all having a whale of a time, and they told me on the last day what a lovely holiday it had been; the Beaconsfield couple, I mean; how they'd recently lost a son in an air accident and felt they had to get away somewhere for a bit, and how the friendship of Alf and Rosie, Joe and Daisy had really lifted them out of the Slough of Despond. I don't mean that you – you know

– should have to endure against your will, and I can get somebody to change seats with you if you'd rather…?'

'No, thanks. I can manage the Alfs of this world. I'm a fully-trained hospital sister.'

'Gosh! Are you really? Then I won't worry. I was in hospital, once, for my tonsils and that Sister was a real old dragon. She was nice-looking, too, but older than you, of course.'

It was much pleasanter meandering through Cornish lanes in the afternoon, with a convoy of private cars eventually tailing the coach, as it was impossible to overtake, but George, the driver kept up a reasonable speed and at the first opportunity drove into a lay-by to allow the queue to pass. Mid-June was not the height of the holiday season and Claire decided she would not have cared to make the journey during August.

'Perhaps you'd like to see Land's End, ladies and gentlemen?' Christine suggested as the coach drew into a parking lot. 'It's not a long walk, and do take heed of all warning notices. Those who prefer to go directly into the restaurant will be provided with afternoon tea on production of the blue tickets provided.'

Claire was surprised when about half the party made directly for the restaurant. Some were approaching elderliness, but none seemed to be halt or lame. Maybe a holiday for them meant continuous refreshments without the preparing or washing up. Land's End was really that. A spectacular peninsular of rocky foot testing the temperature of the thundering, grey Atlantic. As the waves receded she could even count spume-dashed 'toes' occasionally exposed. She walked towards a red notice and leaned against the protective wire to see what lay below.

'Naoh!' came roaring into her ears and she was suddenly grappling with Alf who was shouting, 'Don't do it, darlin'! Don't jump!'

She could hear Joe's ciné camera whirring and sense the breathless expectancy of the two wives awaiting her reaction, and this was to give Alf a good hiding until she looked into his countenance and saw something there which was not brash and loud and intrusive. It was fear hiding behind all his clowning. She had seen that look on the faces of men who had been subjected to severe surgery, and in low, lonely hours of pain just thought they might not make it back to their wives and families on this occasion, and sometimes they were right. Alf Twill was brawny, brassy and a little too ruddy, especially after the mock tussle on the headland. It was not in Claire's province to diagnose but she said, quietly, 'I think you'd better step back, Mr Twill. We're very near the edge, here, and you're much more likely to fall than I am. I have a very good head for heights and I have no intention of jumping.'

Alf backed off with a defensive smile asking, 'You got that, Joey boy? I'm makin' a home movie where I rescue birds in distress. Cor! 'Oo wants Flash Gordon? OK doll?'

The 'doll' gave a brief, dismissive nod and then collected her wits by gazing out to sea again and swallowing her irritation in surveying Nature's majesty. When she eventually scrambled up the path to the road she heard other feet scrambling behind her. Just one pair.

'We're the oddments of the tour,' she pondered, 'and I wonder where *he* does his doctoring?'

After all had partaken of tea the coach had to go back on its tracks for some miles, and then branched off to pass through Bude into Devon, which was also so very lovely scenic-wise. Now Claire was alone, and yet not alone on the double seat, for Doctor Hirst had paused and asked, 'Do you mind–?' eyeing the vacant place beside her.

It was though he was really saying, 'I have noticed that lout, opposite, pestering you and it may be better if I sit here, between you and him,' but she didn't question why so suddenly she seemed to have the power to read people's faces rather than heed their actual words. Her new companion had certainly not pestered her in fifty miles of travelling, apart from asking if she minded him smoking a pipe.

'Not at all,' she said, and found the tobacco smoke quite narcotic. She almost slept at one point.

Ilfracombe, which they reached at eight p.m. was quite delightful, and the sun was turning the Bristol Channel to gold. Some of the livelier members of the tour were planning to dine and then go out on the town; Alf and Co. had already added a couple more souls to their merry clique and spoke of going to the 'Bally' for a 'larf'. Claire pitied the Ballet Company with Alf and Rosie, Joe and Daisy and other such in the audience, but only wanted her bed for her own delectation. Nurses are invariably overworked and the luxury of lying in bed, for such, is underestimated.

The hotel was quite good and sat on a cliff; it boasted home cooking and provided steak and kidney pie for the main course followed by strawberries and Devon Cream. What else? After coffee some people drifted towards the Television lounge, and four played whist, but Claire took her key to room twelve, a single, with a miniscule washbasin, narrow bed and a strip of matting. Another single must be next door for she could hear somebody's tap running and no sooner had her bed creaked than the other bed creaked, too. It was when she smelled the tobacco bearing the name of a saint that she guessed who her neighbour must be.

Lying in bed she reviewed the day. Actually Alf had kept her in such a state of annoyance that she hadn't had time to feel other things, let alone sad. She felt rather pleased that she had got one day over without repining. It hadn't been a bad day, really, and the rest of the company hadn't been at all intrusive. She rather liked Christine, who must be well experienced in welding a party of tourists together, even the odd nuts and bolts such as herself and

Doctor Hirst. With the shush of water breaking against a cliff she fell soundly asleep, and never heard the noisy party returning hilariously from the 'Bally', which was perhaps just as well for all concerned.

TWO

The good weather held and next day broke out of mist into warm sunlight again.

'We're being lucky, weatherwise,' Doctor Hirst said solemnly, as Claire caught his eye while trying to see something of interest the courier was pointing out.

'Aren't we?' she agreed. The coach meandered at a steady forty miles an hour vaguely northwards, girding its loins on patches of motorway to do sixty and then ambling back again on the minor roads. They were to lunch in Gloucester, and then move on through lovely Herefordshire and Shropshire before making a dash through North Wales to Barmouth where their first stopover was. There would be a free day, tomorrow, in Barmouth, and already drifts of conversation were coming from other

31

members of the tour regarding a possible visit to Harlech. Claire would have liked to visit Harlech Castle, redolent of all those doughty men of old, but she still was not ready to be caught up in a mass of humanity. If most of her fellow travellers were going to Harlech then she would find somewhere quiet and maybe just sunbathe, if the fantastic weather still held.

There was no room at the inn for Doctor Hirst when they stopped in Gloucester. Normally tourists who had booked private rooms were also granted private tables at mealtimes, but Christine rather unkindly reminded him that she had told him this might happen at the very start.

'Oh, lord!' he said rather impatiently. 'It's no great matter. What time do you want to move on? I'll go to a pub for a beer and a sandwich.'

'Doctor Hirst–?' Claire never knew why she offered as he was such an unknown quantity he just might have refused. 'Would you care to join me? I don't need a whole table to myself.'

'Thank you.' He sat down and formally introduced himself. 'Robert Hirst,' he said, holding out his hand.

'Claire Matthews,' she responded. Their hands touched briefly as Alf leaned over them.

''Ello, 'ello, 'ello?' he observed. 'First 'e sits wiv 'er, then 'e joins 'er fer lunch an' nah they're 'oldin' 'ands. I arst you, ladies an' gentle*men*, wot next, eh?'

Claire thought of Pete flexing his biceps as Robert Hirst's knuckles showed white for a moment.

'I suppose we're the straight men, so called?' he asked at length with a wry smile. 'People like him have to seek out ready-made butts. I don't know what I'm doing on a coach tour, actually, so I don't want to spoil anyone's fun.'

'Oh, I do,' said Claire. 'I'm astounding myself every minute simply to find myself here. But the scenery's pleasant.'

There was no forced conversation and

when he excused himself to go and smoke a pipe on the terrace she made no move to follow him.

They proceeded through the loveliness of Hereford, with those gorgeous fat, sleek, white-faced cattle regarding them from rich pastures, and then on into Shropshire where they stopped for tea at Much Wenlock.

'Have you read Housman?' asked Robert Hirst.

'Oh, yes. That must be Wenlock Edge, that hill over there. I remember my father reciting a Shropshire Lad to me when I was about twelve and in bed with mumps.'

'Is your father still alive?'

'No. He died five years ago. I never knew my mother. I'm quite, quite alone.'

'It is sometimes better to be alone than lonely, don't you think?'

Claire was so surprised by the passion in the observation that she didn't answer and he had drifted off anyway. She took a little walk, a milky stalk of grass in her mouth and tried to remember the wonderful words her father had recited in his deep voice; she hardly knew she spoke them aloud:

'When I was one-and-twenty
I heard a wise man say,
"Give crowns and pounds and guineas
But not your heart away."'

She paused to sigh. The grass in her mouth oozed sweet sap.

'When I was one-and-twenty
I heard him say again,
"The heart out of the bosom,
was ne'er given in vain.
'Tis paid with sighs a plenty,
And sold for endless rue."
And I am two-and-twenty,
And oh, 'tis true, 'tis true.'

She jumped when a voice spoke from the other side of the wall against which she leant.

'That really sounded as if it came from the

heart, Miss – I mean – Mrs Matthews.'

'Did it, Doctor Hirst? I don't know any other way those particular words can be expressed. But I didn't realize I had an audience. I wasn't intending to follow you.'

'No, forgive me. I'm given to bolting into holes recently. It's as though I don't want to acknowledge that two-and-twenty bit, though I've left it ten years too late.'

She said, very softly, 'You don't owe me any explanations, Doctor Hirst. When you want to talk, I'll listen, and when you want to bolt, go ahead.'

'I feel I should tell you I heard our courier telling the driver you were very young to be a widow. You must often be very lonely, as well as alone. I – I'm sorry. It was clumsy of me just now.'

'Oh, don't worry. Six months have passed, somehow.'

'I lost someone six days ago. Not by death, but as good as.'

'I know words mean very little. But for what they're worth I sympathize. I can promise you things do get better.'

'Thank you. I think we're wanted to continue our Odyssey.'

Christine's voice came clearly, 'Come on, you two! A long way to go before bye-byes.'

Apparently Robert Hirst knew North Wales quite well. He pointed out this and that, a square turreted castle standing on a green hill, a plethora of tiny waterfalls tumbling down a rock face, unpronounceable Welsh town names on signposts and, finally, the estuary of the Dee at Barmouth, tide-full and glistening.

'What are you doing tomorrow?' he asked her over dinner. She had made an effort and dressed in a semi-evening gown as the hotel was quite smart. Her companion, however, didn't seem to have packed a proper suit. He wore a clean shirt with his usual beige velveteen slacks and jacket.

'I'm sorry,' he had said when she appeared. 'I got on the 'bus just as I was. I feel positively *deshabille* beside you.'

'I'm not one who believes clothes makes

the man,' she had tried to put him at ease. 'I'm going to hear a Welsh choir with my father's ex-curate after dinner. I wasn't quite sure what to wear for such an event.'

'Oh, I'm sure you'll do very well.'

Now she said, thoughtfully, 'Tomorrow? I haven't thought about it seriously. I know I'm *not* joining the party going to Harlech. I may just look around this place. I don't know Wales at all.'

'Well, if you would like to see something rather stunning, and care for a bit of a scramble, I'm climbing Cader Idris tomorrow. It's quite easy if you have strong shoes, or you can hire boots from the hotel porter. Of course only if you feel like stretching yourself after all that sitting down. You may prefer to rest. If you're not around at eight a.m. I'll know you're not coming.'

'Well, thanks,' Claire said promptly. 'We'll leave it at that then, shall we? I haven't climbed anything since the year I took "A" levels. I celebrated with some friends a week in the Pyrenées.'

'Cader Idris is a molehill by Pyrenean standards, but it can be heavy going through the bogs.'

She awoke at seven next morning feeling as bright as a button and somehow on a note of expectancy. Ah! it was just that Doctor Hirst had offered to take her climbing or – in his words – scrambling if she cared to accompany him. That was all. Nothing really exciting. Still – she lifted the telephone by her bed and ordered a continental-type breakfast in her room, a luxury which would cost her an extra thirty pence, she read on a wall notice, but would keep her free of the main party while they breakfasted. She nipped along to a bathroom and showered, and when she returned the tray was awaiting her; the coffee smelling particularly delicious. Now what had made her pack a pair of jeans? she wondered. She donned these with a blue, long-sleeved blouse and tied a cardigan round her neck. Then she ate the light breakfast with appetite. The trip must be doing her good as she was beginning to enjoy her food again.

So far the sun wasn't shining, but it wasn't looking like rain, either. A sort of sea-mist blotted out the landscape into substantial greyness.

She descended the stairs and asked for the hall-porter. He was breakfasting, she was told, so she waited until he reappeared at eight and asked to hire some boots. She had long, slim feet, but with two pairs of borrowed socks she was eventually ready. It was now ten past eight and it looked as though Robert Hirst had left without her, but disappointment failed to register with her after all she had been through. It would have been nice to climb a mountain but maybe she could go for a walk on her own.

'Are you ready, Mrs Matthews?'

She gazed at the stranger uncomprehendingly. He was tall with a thick mane of leonine hair and clear, periwinkle-blue eyes. He was dressed seriously for climbing, in breeches and knee-length hose. Another pair of socks were turned over his stout boots. His polo-necked pullover was the colour of his eyes.

'Don't tell me it makes that much difference?' he asked, and ran an investigating finger over his cheek and chin.

'Doctor Hirst?' she actually laughed. 'I should just say it does! You've shaved all that hair off your face! In a way I'm sad, but it does make you look years younger.'

She could hardly believe that her heart felt lighter that he had waited for her. She *was* really looking forward to the day ahead now.

She helped him shoulder a heavy haversack.

'Do I need one of those?' she asked.

'No.' He gave her a brief appraisal from head to foot which made her colour up, slightly, because she still hadn't got used to his changed appearance. Robert Hirst was a handsome man by any standards. 'You look quite adequate. I should roll your pants up a bit. I have a spare mac and sou'wester should we need one up there, and food and drink also. I think when the tide goes out, however, we're in for another hot day. I'm counting on it because I want to show you an unforgettable view which is lost in cloudy conditions.'

They walked six miles in the first hour, and were on the lower slopes of the mountain. Claire was already gasping.

'Gosh! But I'm unfit!' she laughed apologetically. 'What must you be thinking of me! I don't want to hold you back. I would honestly like you to go on without me if you'd rather. I can wander back at my leisure.'

'Rubbish! I'm used to walking and I probably pushed the pace a bit. We have all day and we'll go slowly, slowly and maybe catch a few monkeys.'

She laughed again and he actually smiled back at her.

'Here! sit down for a ten minute breather on this boulder. Ah! here comes the sun. I thought he might.'

She breathed clean exhilarating air as though she had just discovered it and watched the mists being eaten up as though into some giant maw.

'I can see, now, I've been like a worm, who has done only what was necessary to exist and crept away, between times, into the dark. Rather like you and your bolt-holes.'

'Would you care to talk about it? How did it happen?'

'He killed himself in his car. A party – too much to drink – but fortunately nobody else was involved. I was making curtains when I was told. They never did get finished, let alone put up.'

'Thanks for telling me.'

'Thank *you* for listening. I've never discussed it with anybody before. I didn't think I could. I must be getting better.'

'I hope so. It was you who told me one did.'

'Would it help to – talk about your trouble?'

She wondered if she had gone too far too

soon when he took his time stuffing his pipe and lighting up with great deliberation. He exhaled fragrant smoke and then looked over her shoulder.

'It was a girl, of course,' he said, slowly, as though every word was a stone he had to expel from his mouth. 'The wedding was arranged in a bit of a rush. She didn't show up on the day, or 'phone. Next day I got a "Dear John" letter, as I believe the Americans call them, telling me she was sorry but she was going off with Kevin, and would be marrying him as soon as he was free.' He looked down at his sturdy boots and wriggled his feet as though to assure himself that they were his. 'Those are the plain facts. I think only somebody like you could appreciate that they open the gates to a sort of private hell. God! I don't even know who Kevin is! I should do, because I thought I knew her so well. So after stumbling about from hotel to hotel for days I finally got on that damned 'bus. Or maybe that's too vehement. I may quite like the 'bus after two weeks, and it's not costing as much as hotels.'

'You have no home then?' Claire asked quietly.

'Oh, lord, yes, I have a home, *and* parents; two brothers and a sister, too. But would *you* want to rush home with such a tale?'

'They – weren't at the wedding, then? I m – mean, they weren't at the church, or–?'

'I told you the wedding was planned in a rush. It was arranged at a Register Office and would have been a surprise to most of our relatives and friends. There was a reason for haste.' He began to knock out his pipe on a stone and Claire knew that he didn't want to talk any more just then. She was not surprised when he said, 'Ready to push on a bit?' and reached out his hand to haul her to her feet. 'Shout if you get tired before I suggest stopping again.'

The stony track ran out soon after and Claire put a foot with a squelch into her first bog.

'I suppose people don't disappear in these

things?' she asked, at length.

'Not usually,' he turned to smile. 'Take long, slow strides. You'll find you get the hang of it very quickly.'

Suck! Plop! she heard her feet going underneath her, and found herself thinking about his story. He possibly thought she didn't understand the pain and humiliation of rejection, though she might understand the finality of loss. But she did understand quite a bit, though she had never liked to admit it even to herself. Pete, who had been so popular, had also been extremely popular with women. He had once or twice, to her knowledge, broken dates with her to spend with other women, and lied about these occasions. Her finding out about them had been accidental and then he had been anxious only to be forgiven. 'You do trust me, Sweetie, don't you? I mean, if you don't, there's no point–' But she had never put *him* to such tests of loyalty. There was nobody she even cared to look at while Pete was around.

'Well? How was that?' Robert Hirst asked her eventually, so that she jumped and realized they were once more on solid ground.

'Oh!' she looked behind her. 'Have we really climbed all that way up? I must have got my second wind, or something. My! That's some view!'

'It's even better from the top,' he decided, 'though now the scrambling starts that I promised you. Still game?'

'Game!' she agreed, and laughed a little.

He said, still surveying the distant hamlets and midget cars with sun-sparkle on their windscreens, 'It did help telling someone about my trouble. I feel quite unburdened.'

'I'm glad,' she said, 'I'm sure, now, I went the wrong way about things, trying to keep everything bottled up and out of sight. Behaving like an alcoholic, I suppose.'

'What a splendid analogy! Perhaps, in my own case, all I'm really suffering from is humiliation. Obviously this Kevin had something for Angela I don't possess.

People speak far too glibly about broken hearts. Hearts are extremely resilient.'

'I agree,' she said from the heart which had surprised her by its resilience.

'So excelsior, yes?'

'Excelsior! Excelsior!' she cried, and found an echo. She tried again and her voice rolled round and round the surrounding hills. He saw her with her hands cupping her lips, her eyes closed the better to hear, showing long, dark curling lashes against her pale cheeks, the ribbon tying her hair coming loose and blowing in the mountain breeze and he smiled.

'That is called making the Welkin ring, I believe,' he smiled. 'What a lovely word Welkin is! By the way, how was your choir last evening?'

'Marvellous. They certainly would make any Welkin ring. After you, Doctor Hirst,' and she waved vaguely upwards.

'Would it be an awful imposition to call you Claire? And for you to call me Robert, or Rob? I don't want to appear pushing–'

'No, that's quite all right, Rob. I'll call you Rob, if you don't mind. I already know quite a few Roberts.'

'Then come on, Claire. Dig your toes in when you climb and shout for a hand if you need one.'

A really breathless, exhilarating three quarters of an hour passed for her, as they scrambled up a dried up stream-bed, rounded a stony outcrop of rock and then tried to get purchase on a loose bed of shale.

'Oops!' she called out as she felt herself slipping.

'Watch it, Claire!' as he reached out for her hand they both looked down and saw the blood seeping through her socks and down into her boot. 'I'm sorry!' he said. 'Slate can be as sharp as a knife. You're not the fainting type, are you? Because we ought to get to the top and then look at that. Sideways up a scree, Claire. I should have told you. It's a bit like walking on skis.'

'I haven't done that, either, and I'm not a fainting type. I'm a trained nurse.'

'Oh!' He sounded a bit odd as they reached a flat ledge. 'Then maybe you'd like to attend to yourself? Here's the first-aid box.'

She took off her boot and then her socks. The slate had gone in quite deeply and the sight of her own blood still gushing out, the wound disturbed, no doubt, by her actions, made her feel a little odd.

'Rob!' she said, 'would you see to me, please?'

He handed her a small bottle of Sal Volatile and pressed a clean dressing firmly over the wound until the bleeding had stopped. He then replaced the pad and rather clumsily bandaged the whole. 'No, let me,' he said as she reached for her socks, which he turned and replaced, finally pulling on her borrowed boot. 'All right?' he asked. 'You looked a bit pale for a moment there.'

'I felt a bit pale. I'm ashamed of myself. A tough, hospital sister I call myself, and then I get a prick and I'm all of a dither.'

'More of a stab than a prick. We're only a hundred yards, or so, from our luncheon spot. Don't argue. I'm going to carry you. We don't want to start the bleeding off again and after an hour you should be fine.'

She felt rather dreamlike, finding herself held close to the blue pullover and trying not to look into the equally-blue eyes, in fact deliberately trying not to read anything into the situation which couldn't be there. Even so alien thoughts intruded, like, 'Isn't he strong? He picked me up as though I was a child;' and 'He must have been a beautiful blond child. He's still quite blond. The Viking type. They carried girls off, too.'

The last thought made her wriggle a little, mentally before it became physical, and by that time he had set her down in an enclosed valley, with the cone of the mountain still enclosing them.

'I'll go back for the rucksack,' he said, 'and I think you had a cardigan, Claire. You'll need it up there.' He pointed towards the summit. 'We're making for that. It's quite

51

easy, really. No more scree.'

He disappeared and she looked around. How peaceful it was here and how remote from the world which was out there somewhere! It was warm with the sea-breeze cut off and she saw unknown mountain flowers growing in crevices and grasses growing where surely there could be no moisture to nurture them?

Rob unpacked lunch; he even spread a small chequered cloth and laid out meat-paste sandwiches and cold sausages and tomatoes and a flask of hot, steaming tea.

'How absolutely lovely and I'm famished!' she exclaimed. 'I don't know when I was so hungry!'

'Climb a few more mountains, Claire,' he advised. 'They're good for the appetite.'

They ate companionably, watched a soaring bird of prey and wondered if there were eagles hereabouts. Rob brought forth dessert, fresh peaches, and refilled the cups with the last of the tea.

'Now after this we have a bottle of water,

only, and if required. There's a nice little pub on the road back where we can stop for tea.'

'I can't imagine wanting anything else today, Rob. But you seem to know this area pretty well. I'll take your word for it that mountains are good for the appetite, and wait and see.' She leaned back to watch a cloud swan float overhead and change into a windblown little ship on a heavenly ocean. 'There's a kind of – of magic here,' she decided. 'Do you feel it?'

'It's funny you should say that,' he observed, 'because it was in my mind at that moment to ask if you could ever bring yourself to believe in fairies?'

She looked from the sky into the sharp blue of his eyes and laughed aloud. Another of those alien thoughts intruded that she hadn't thought much about Pete, today, but that she would make up for it later.

'Fairies?' she echoed. 'Once I did, of course, but I think a nurse's training does rather inhibit the imagination. One has to absorb so many hard facts. Why did you ask?'

'I always think about fairies when I'm up here, on this mountain, which can be very, very magical, I agree with you. My father was an Air Force officer in the last war, and I grew up loving his tales of the goings-on in the Squadron. For a while he was based not far from here and my favourite story is of the two young sergeant-pilots, who were chalk and cheese to look at but David and Jonathan in their liking of each other; real pals, who liked to go climbing when they could between sorties. One was clean-cut, good-looking, well-spoken and the other a real son of the soil, a farmer's son with a weatherworn face and bright, ginger hair. Well Connie – short for Connington – and Ginger decided to climb the mountain during a weekend's leave, and had got to about where we are, now, when a storm broke, and the heavens were opened. The thunder rolled and the lightning danced from rock to rock – I've seen it and it does make you think you're in the presence of divine anger – but when the rain came down the two lads made off in opposite directions looking for shelter. Connie could only find a bit of grassy overhang, like that bit over there, and this soon dripped as badly as the rain so that he got soaked to the skin. When the rain stopped he shouted rudely for Ginger to show himself, and when he did he was bone dry and sort of far away. Connie asked where he'd been and Ginger said he'd been in a cave and met a fairy. Well, Connie couldn't stop laughing while he was wringing out his shirt and shorts and Ginger went very quiet and said he wouldn't discuss the matter any more. Connie said, "Oh, come on, Ginger! You don't expect me to believe that rubbish?" Ginger said he could please himself because the fairy had told him nobody would believe him and it was better to save his breath. Connie thought he'd better humour his pal, because he did seem to be a bit odd, so he asked what the fairy was like. "Beautiful," said

Ginger, going all enthusiastic. "She was wearing a sort of rainbow for a dress and she kissed me and said if I wished hard enough we could always be together. There was a pool in the cave with goldfish swimming in it and little silver frogs jumping up and down, too. It was like nothing you ever saw." "And this all happened in a cave?" Connie asked, trying to keep his patience. "Yes, and it wasn't no ordinary cave, mate. This was furnished like a palace." "Right," said Connie, "so it can't be far away. You didn't get rained on, so show me." Ginger said, "I dunno as I oughter – I kinda gathered it was between me an' – an' 'er." "This *fairy*?" said Connie. "I might – I just might believe you, Ginge, if I see the cave. But don't push me too far. I've got to see *something*." So Ginger led the way and they looked, but there was no cave, not even a hollow where Ginger might have sheltered from the rain. They found not a thing, and yet Connie was still soaking and his pal as dry as a bone. Not even a hair of his head was wet. Connie got a bit impatient and accused his pal of being bonkers, but Ginger just remarked that the fairy said other people *would* react like that, and it would be better not to mention it. "I wish you hadn't," said Connie, "because I can just see myself telling the C.O. my friend has just seen a ruddy fairy!" Well, after that, they got different postings and lost touch, but Connington met my father years afterwards and told him this story, and its sequel. It appears that Ginger got a job as instructor at a private flying club, and one day, when conditions became unsuitable for flying, Ginger took up an old 'plane to guide a young weekend-flier back to the club, and when he had shepherded the lad in he unaccountably took off westwards. Nobody saw him again. There were no reports of a crashed 'plane or wreckage ever found. As Ginger was an orphan, by this time, and had never married, there wasn't much of a to-do. In such a light 'plane he couldn't even have made Ireland, let alone defected behind the iron curtain, and he was going the wrong way, anyhow, to do that. Well Connington, for auld lang syne, took his family to Wales for a holiday and they mooched around here much as we're doing, now. It came on to rain and they dashed down to the road, where Connington was stopped by an old woman. "Did you find a 'plane, sir?" she asked him. "Up there?" and she looked up at the mountain. "A 'plane?" Connie asked. "Up there? No. Why? Is there one?" "I saw it," she said. "It came over in the thunder and the mountain opened to receive it. I've told 'em. But they don't believe me. They won't believe you, either." Connie said his wife called out from the car, "For God's sake, Jack, come out of the rain! You're getting soaked." "The old woman kept me," he explained. "What old woman?" she asked. "The old woman I was talking to. The one who looked like a witch." His wife looked at him very oddly and said, "There *was* no old woman, Jack. You stood there on your own, looking up at the mountain, talking to yourself. You are an idiot sometimes, you know." Connington drove away as fast as he dare and that's about the end of the story.'

Claire glanced around her.

'You *are* pulling my leg, aren't you?' she asked.

'In so far as yarns are passed down from father to son, no, I'm not,' he smiled. 'Connie and Ginger were real people, and Connington only came out with the full story after his own rather weird experience. I, personally, rather like to think of Ginger and his Welsh Fairy living happily ever after somewhere.'

'Probably in that cave!' Claire's eyes lit up. 'Do you think *we* might find it?'

'The cave? I've looked ever since I first heard the story.'

'Then does that mean you half believe in it?'

'I would like to. Aren't we always saying wonders will never cease? Why should they?'

She began helping him to pack up, finding him a most entertaining companion. When he put his hand to his ear and asked 'Fairies?' she laughed as a party of young climbers clumped across the rocky arena, calling out greetings in German.

'Entschuldigen Sie uns, bitte,' called the leader. 'Zat is please to pardon–'

'Ich verstehe Sie. Die Berge sind frei für all.'

'Sie sprechen Deutsch, ja?'

'Nur Hoch deutsch. Ich denke Sie aus der Schweiz gekommen sind?'

'Sie haben rechts.' The party laughed. 'Vielleicht werden wir Sie in die Schweiz sehen kommen?'

'Vielleicht,' Robert added.

'Unsere Berge sind grösser als diese Berge, nich wahr?'

Everybody laughed.

'Wir verlassen Sie mit Ihrer Verlobt.'

Robert looked at Claire who had only understood an odd word here and there.

'Sie ist nicht meine Verlobt; sondern eine Bekannte.'

Claire knew by the attention she was

getting, as she tied her ribbon round her hair, that she was the subject of the parting joke shared by everyone else, even Rob.

'What was all that about?' she asked. 'You seem to be quite a German speaker. I never got my der – die – das quite sorted out.'

'Well they were Swiss, actually, from the German-speaking north. One can tell if an English-speaking person comes from north of the Border or Southend. They hoped they would see us in Switzerland. I said perhaps, and they then remarked with great joy that their mountains were a bit bigger than ours.' Claire was smiling. 'They then said they'd leave me alone with my fianceé. I pointed out you were not my fianceé but an acquaintance, then some wag said that many acquaintances went up into the mountains, back home, and came down engaged to be married.'

'Oh! So that's what all the jollity was about!'

'They meant no harm.'

'Oh, gracious, I'm not offended. I'm

rather glad to be your Be – what was it?'

'Bekannte. Even after that bit about what could happen on the way down.'

'I think we must be the only two people hereabouts absolutely safe from that possibility. Don't you? Knowing what we know about each other is why we're together. We're both immunised from that sort of involvement. I'm enjoying the day, though, Rob. It's rather nice not to feel emotional about someone.'

'Then let us make the top.' He glanced at his watch. 'The time should be just right.'

They climbed in a zig-zag and half an hour later he held out his hand indicatively. 'There you are! That's the crock of gold at the end of this particular rainbow. What do you think?'

THREE

Though the sun was hot the breeze was
rough here on the summit and tore at
Claire's hair as she looked down on an
unforgettable sight. The Barmouth Estuary
lay below, the tide fast receding oceanwards
in a grey-silver wash, and leaving behind it
an expanse of golden sand gem-studded
with iridescent pools, each individually
shaded and resembling an opal. The effect
of the sun, the deep-blue sky, the cotton-
wool clouds on the breeze-ruffled waters
had to be seen to be believed.

'It's worth the climb, isn't it?' Rob asked.

'I should say it is. Oh, Rob, it's so beautiful
I want to cry. I don't know what it is up here,
whether one feels closer to God, or not, but
I want to say it'll be all right, Rob, for both
of us. I feel sure and I want you to know.'

'Thank you, Claire.' He took her hand and kissed it sexlessly. 'Up here I can believe odd things, too. That we were meant to meet, perhaps? To – to comfort each other.'

'I hope so. I do indeed.'

'Now we go down, the shortest way,' he said at length.

'Is there a short way?'

'Would you like to find that out by starting to roll?'

She laughed and he offered his hand.

'Come on, Bekannte, take proffered help. Sometimes unexercised muscles can't cope so well with a descent.'

In just over half an hour, having taken full advantage of her companion's help, Claire found herself cutting across a field with a road at the bottom.

'Ten minutes to the pub,' Rob told her. 'How's your appetite?'

'I think I could manage another cuppa. Maybe bread and jam and scones and – and cake. Not much more.'

They both laughed.

'And you've enjoyed it, eh?'

'I have. Thanks for dragging me along.'

'It was my pleasure. When I saw that view for the first time as a young undergrad I was going through a poetical phase. I had to get the experience into words. I've forgotten the actual opus only that I declaimed how I had climbed to knock upon the door of very heaven and seen it, instead, far below at a mountain's foot, forever forbidden to man, for the nearer one approached the further the illusion drifted. It's true, you know. At ground level the estuary is just any old stretch of sand with the flotsam and jetsam of the tide despoiling it.'

Alf and Co. were awaiting the couple's arrival, in a prominent position propping up the hotel bar.

'Nah then! Nah then!' Alf said saucily. 'Who's bringing yer home ternight, darlin'? Well, I never! It's the ruddy Doc come out from under all the undergrowth. You see, Dais? Quite a good lookin' feller, our Doc is. You been behavin' yourselves, have yer?

65

A likely tale!'

For a moment Claire felt the old desire to freeze in embarrassment and then she heard Rob laugh out loud.

'Come on!' he said, chummily, drawing her up to the bar. 'What's everybody having? This round's on me.'

There was to be a two day stopover in the Lake District, and for the first time conditions were cloudy with a threat of rain as they neared their hotel base in Ambleside.

'It can do this so easily, hereabouts,' Rob said, peering past Claire into the gloom as they eased past banks of incredible rhododendrons bordering the hotel drive. 'I think if it's fine tomorrow we should take advantage and climb Helvellyn; I'll guide you along Striding Edge if you're game.'

Claire said, however, 'Not tomorrow, Rob. I've already made plans.'

He looked stunned for a moment and then said quickly, 'Of course. I understand.

Excuse me.'

She saw him helping the driver to unload and distribute the luggage and carry it into the hotel lobby. She hoped to catch him to have a word, but he was quickly busy carrying Mrs Font's and Miss Durrant's luggage upstairs for them. They had shared an interesting day's conversation, especially when they travelled for many miles along a motorway, and she had been glad of a day's inactivity to allow her muscles to recover. Her thighs were just a little stiff today.

'He thinks I snubbed him,' Claire fretted as she showered in her self-contained room. 'I shouldn't have been quite so abrupt.'

She actually thought he wasn't coming in to dinner as she arrived at the table for two and he wasn't there. He had not come after a further ten minutes.

'You two 'ad a rah, or somefink?' Alf wanted to know.

'No. Of course not.' She said quickly, and looked quite cheered when Rob spoke from above her.

'Good evening, Claire. Hungry?'

'Not so hungry as last night. I haven't been climbing mountains,' and she smiled.

He seemed to have been shopping as he was wearing a grey lounge suit, collar and tie.

'Off the peg,' he indicated his clothes, 'from Monsieur Burton's shop in Windermere. That's just my excuse if it doesn't fit properly. I rather felt I was letting the side down as the ruffian of the party.'

'Actually you look very nice, Rob,' she said sincerely. 'You do something for Burton's. You should ask for a discount.'

While they were being so nice and on an impersonal plane he said, quietly, 'I apologize for behaving as though you were my exclusive preserve, Claire, and planning your days to fit in with mine, like an obedient oriental wife.' He took a spoonful of the excellent onion soup.

'I should love to climb Helvellyn with you on Thursday, Rob,' she told him, 'if – if conditions are favourable, of course. I have no other plans apart from tomorrow and I'm most grateful for your company, as I thought you knew. My in-laws live at Penrith, which I believe can be reached easily from Windermere. I felt I owed them a visit in the circumstances. We haven't met since the funeral. You – you do understand?'

'Of course. It must be rather a trial for you in anticipation. Was he their only son?'

'Yes. They have a married daughter living in Newcastle, I believe.'

So it was that Claire found herself gazing at sombre stone villages and little towns from the train window and being frowned on by the purple peaks of the Cumbrian landscape. It was a lowering day, rather depressing after all the loveliness June had earlier provided, but shortly after eleven the sun broke through and the stone town of Penrith smiled a welcome through its tears. Everything was so clean, Claire decided; the streets as though washed, the houses boasting pretty curtains and smart paint-work. As a southerner born and bred, Claire had always imagined the north to be a place of satanic mills and chimneys belching smoke, but Penrith surprised her with its gentility. She wouldn't be surprised if everybody hereabouts rode to hounds, or would they be on foot, as John Peel had been?

She took a taxi out to Meldrum: the taxi driver knew the house without further information. Claire began to feel shy as on the outskirts of the town they turned into a wide drive and approached a square, solid-looking house. She had only met the Matthews parents once before the marriage, and that had been at a celebratory party in London. She could tell Mrs Matthews thought they had hasted a little to the wedding. 'You should have given us more warning, dear. It's a long way to come, you know,' and at the funeral nobody had had much to say at all. When Claire had asked if they would care to sleep at the cottage Mr Matthews had thanked her but said no, they would stay at a hotel. Jane, their daughter, was due to be confined and he added that the living must always come first.

It was Jane who flung open the door, a tall young woman in a kaftan with a cigarette in a holder clenched between her teeth.

'My sister-in-law, I believe?' she greeted, without removing this, offering a long, limp hand. 'Come in, do! I don't know what you saw in that brother of mine. He was the absolute bottom.'

Claire didn't know whether to smile or frown at this as Mrs Matthews swept forward to embrace her.

'How are you, dear? How nice of you to come and see us! I was so surprised when you 'phoned from Wales.'

'Actually Mum was surprised you were recovered enough to take a holiday,' Jane decided. 'Pete's widow was expected to remain in a state of perpetual mourning, yet here you are gadding around the country and looking quite blooming.'

'I wouldn't say gadding, exactly,' protested Claire. 'I was due for leave and I'm on a coach tour. How's the baby?'

'Baby Pete? Fine. You see when I had a boy he *had* to be Pete. At least *I* remained faithful to memory.'

'Take no notice of Jane,' said Mrs Matthews, towing Claire away into the drawing-room where a plump, rosy-cheeked girl served coffee. 'She has always been difficult and is being difficult now, which is why she's here with me instead of at home with her husband.'

'Odd how you managed to have difficult children, isn't it?' Jane asked, quite un-abashed. 'There was Pete, always chasing girls – sorry, Claire, but he *was* my wayward brother – and me so plain I couldn't get a feller. Only when Daddy provided the dowry of that job in Newcastle did Johnny look at me a second time and we nabbed him. And look what a fine old mess all that is turning out to be!'

Claire was feeling terribly embarrassed by all this. She had the feeling that Mrs Matthews, whose manners were impeccable, was really very angry, as she had suspected she was irritated and angry as she had spoken at the wedding of wishing there had been more notice of the young couple's plans.

'How is – is your husband?' she asked, to cover her uneasiness. She couldn't have called him 'Father' for the world.

'James is very well. He's a County Councillor, you know, and they're having a big meeting today. He asked to be excused. My dear–' she looked gravely and considerately at Claire – 'it's been six long months now. You must eventually think of marrying again. Is there–?'

'What she means is don't you dare!' Jane cut in. 'When Pete honoured you above all women you became blessed. Do you feel blessed?'

'I feel a bit out of my depth now that I am here,' Claire said, and decided to take charge of the situation. 'I don't want you to try to spoil the little Pete and I had, Jane, by trying to belittle either him or me. If you're unhappy, I'm sorry, but like the sickest person on the ward you mustn't be allowed to drag everybody else down. Maybe I'll marry again one day, and maybe not. I have no plans at present other than to get a new job.'

'That's called cutting one down to size,' Jane said with a shrug and lit another cigarette. 'She's going to be tougher than you thought isn't she, Mother, darling? She may escape this family altogether if you don't watch out.'

'Where were you thinking of working, dear?' asked Mrs Matthews. 'Didn't Peter leave you properly provided for?'

Claire swallowed. Was Pete supposed to have had money, then? If so it hadn't been squandered on her.

'As a trained nurse I feel I ought to work,' she hedged the question. 'I haven't decided where.'

'James has some influence in the County. We have some very fine hospitals.'

'Go on! Go on!' urged Jane.

'I had thought I might go abroad,' said Claire, who had had no such idea until that very moment.

'Oh! Alas and alack!' jeered Jane. 'You don't want to stay in this magic family circle?'

'Jane! Would you go upstairs and see to your child?' Mrs Matthews asked with that same cold, polite anger which froze.

'Why should I? Lizzie can do that.'

'Lizzie is preparing luncheon.'

'Oh, then I'd better go and do it myself, Mummy, hadn't I?'

Claire found herself on her feet. Actually she would have liked to run away but held on to herself.

'May I come with you, Jane?' she asked feeling she preferred the obvious barbs of the daughter to the hidden arrows in the Mother's quiver.

'Of course, if you want to. See little Petey, eh? Actually he's quite a nice little kid. He deserves a better family. Would you care to adopt him? I should think, in spite of my brother, you're really quite unspoilt.'

Of that whole day, which Claire endured because she knew in her secret heart she could never repeat it, the only bits which were remotely tolerable were those spent with the six month old Petey, a sturdy little child who looked as though he would grow up to resemble his demised uncle. When he needed changing, she offered to change him, and during the afternoon accompanied Jane on a pram-pushing expedition to a very pretty park. Later she felt she owed her mother-in-law an hour of her time, and so sat with that lady on the south-facing terrace of the house, drinking tea and hearing of the devotion between mother and son, which no other woman could be expected to understand, and consequently the loss which had blighted her life for ever, again an experience no other woman could ever share.

'I was somewhat blighted by losing Pete, myself, you know,' Claire felt bound to interpolate.

'Oh, my dear! Of course. Love is very physical at that stage, though, isn't it? You were *in love* with Pete. What woman in her right mind wouldn't be? He left half a dozen broken hearts round here, I may tell you. But a mother's love is – is–'

'Doesn't your mother love take comfort in Jane? She seems to be very brittle and unhappy.'

'Jane is – Jane. She revels in causing havoc for some reason. I have tried to understand her but she doesn't want to be understood. Now if you had left Peter for me and Jane had been taken–'

All this delivered almost in a monotone made Claire think she was on another planet.

'*I* didn't kill Pete,' she said in a voice which quivered, and ignoring the second part of the statement. 'You know he was driving while he was drunk. You read the coroner's report as I did.'

'But why should he be drunk on his wedding day, when he was not in your company? Why did you not keep him close to you as any warm-blooded woman would have done on such a day? Could you be frigid, Claire, to drive my son to drink and to his end?'

Claire had never known there was something of the harridan in her nature. She spoke, and supplied all the emotion lacking in Mrs Matthews' evenly-modulated tones.

'I wasn't with him because there was an emergency at the hospital, and half the staff were down with 'flu. After the service we both had to go back on duty and I finished at five o'clock. Pete was through about an hour later, and because there had been no stag-party, owing to this self-same emergency, a few of the staff dragged him off to the pub. He probably only meant to have a couple of drinks, because he would be well aware that I was waiting for him, and despite your maternal devotion and all his other conquests, it *was* me he was *in love* with at that time, physically, mentally, emotionally – the lot. But your son could be weak, Mrs Matthews, and obviously gave in when somebody said, "Have another one, Pete," and "One for the road, Pete," until he was absolutely sozzled, despite all that devotion waiting for him at home in the cottage. And as to your final question, Mrs Matthews, it's none of your damned business. I would suggest you put your own house in order before you dare to question mine!'

At the finish she was almost screaming with passion, while tears ran unchecked down her face.

'Welcome to the club,' came Jane's amused, brittle voice. 'In time everybody likes to tell Mother off, though she got you rattled rather more quickly than the rest, no doubt because she knows you're escaping her clutches. The only thing is that it all rolls off her like water off a duck's back. Displays of emotion are akin to see-through nighties in mother's book. I'm always vaguely amazed that Pete and I got born at all. Out of love and passion? Never! Mother is incapable of the first and believes the second to be definitely indecent. Want another hankie, Claire?'

'Thanks.'

'I really don't know what all that was about,' said Mrs Matthews, reaching to pick up a length of crochetwork, and behaving as though her daughter was invisible, 'but if it did you any good, my dear, to get things off your chest, well I don't mind your un-graciousness in screaming at me one little bit.'

'Yes, I *am* sorry about that,' Claire said, under control once more. 'I shouldn't have lost my temper in your house. But what I said is true and what is also true is that I wish I hadn't come. I don't know what I expected of Pete's family, but it certainly wasn't be brutalized by any member of it. I think there's a train a five-thirty. Would you allow me to telephone for a taxi, please?'

'No need for that,' Jane said quickly. 'I'll run you to the station in my car, Claire, then

I think I'll return to the lesser evil, my own husband. Is that all right, Mother?'

'You must do exactly as you want, Jane. You always have.'

In the car Jane became a little more human, and asked to be forgiven for her part in the day's 'shenanigens', her own word for events.

'You wouldn't have stood a chance with Mother on your own,' she said confidently, 'she's like water on stone and one gets worn down unknowingly. I actually did you a favour by putting you on your guard. "Oh," I could hear you thinking, "what an awful sister Pete had! What an absolute bitch! She doesn't deserve a lovely little boy like Petey and he doesn't deserve her." Well, I'll you, Claire, I do, and he's going to be loved as I never was, but not smothered as befell his uncle and namesake.'

'And is it true your marriage isn't happy?'

'Of course not. It's not idyllic but it's normally contented. Johnny's mad about Petey, too. But it suits my book to play up the misery so that Mother's out of a job. You must find all this absolutely unbeliveable, Claire?'

'My head's in a whirl.'

'Oh, and look! Damn! The station car-park's full. All the dutiful wives must be waiting for their loving husbands. I can't get any nearer, Claire, so you just rush. Just go. No time for goodbyes. Good luck!'

Though Claire ran she missed the train back to Windermere, and there wasn't another for two hours. She wandered outside, bought a local paper and desultorily, over a cup of tea, read about fell races and hound-trails and lakeland wrestling in a kind of daze. She still heard Mrs Matthews' one-key voice sounding in her inner ear, and the words eating into her brain like a maggot. 'Could you be frigid, Claire, to drive my son to drink and to his end?'

By the time the slow, stopping train arrived she had a headache and was glad simply to slip into a corner and close her eyes. The gloom in which she had left

Windermere bathed did not appear to have lifted, and it was still gloomy and the night ahead held a threat of depression.

Her spirits lifted briefly as she beheld Rob Hirst apparently awaiting her.

'They said this was the last train.' He took one look at her face and offered his arm. 'Bad, was it?'

'I – I can't talk about it just yet, Rob, if you don't mind.'

'No. All right. I've got the hotel station-wagon outside. The porter's having a night off and he told me to use it. I take it you don't want to face our lot en masse? Alf, Joe and Co., are having a darts party. Miss Durrant is quite a dab hand.'

'I would like to go straight to bed.'

'Right. I'll do a recce and see you get straight upstairs. On condition you allow me to have a tray sent up. You have a lean and hungry look and things always seem better on a full stomach.'

She managed a little smile.

'I needed a friend just then, when I got

back,' she said. 'How did you know?'

'A fellow-feeling, maybe–?'

Impulsively she reached out and put a hand over his on the steering wheel. There were no words but after a brief communion she sighed and let him drive on unhampered.

'Goodnight and thanks,' she said as he waved her upstairs towards her bedroom at the hotel. 'I'm sorry to be a misery.'

'You're not. I'll see you tomorrow.'

FOUR

Claire had not enjoyed the best of nights but she awoke with a determination not to retrogress further in the business of getting over Pete's death. The previous day she had become emotionally so outraged that she craved only peace and tranquility today. Much as one hesitates to stir up the nerve in a bad tooth, which is temporarily easy, she wanted to enter into absolute normality and try to forget memories which were abhorrent to her. She appeared at the breakfast table opposite Rob looking almost unnaturally radiant, her eyes bright as diamonds and her mouth smiling. He was a little surprised that she was wearing make-up so early in the day; usually she was a girl – he couldn't think of her as a widowed woman – whose natural assets were such as needed little aid, but now he saw the carefully painted blue shading above her eyes, which was attractive and successfully disguised the natural bruising which lay faintly below. There was a blush of pink on her cheeks, though he knew that even in health she was naturally pale, and she had dressed her hair in two braids which she wore like a coronet.

'Good morning, Claire!' he greeted, having risen to see her seated. 'You look gorgeous.'

'Thank you, Rob!' She glanced up at him and away again. The coquettishness of this intrigued him. If he had thought he was getting to know her, this morning she was a completely mystery to him.

Alf called out, in form, as usual.

'Hi, doll, ah 'baht you and me getting' lorst terday, eh? I bin very patient wiv you up to nah!'

'Another time, Alf, I'd love to, if Rosie approves. But today I think we're climbing a mountain. Aren't we, Rob?'

Those brilliant eyes hit his so sharply there was almost a tinkling of broken glass.

'Are we?' he asked seriously. 'Are you sure you're up to it?'

'Of course I'm up to it. I'm looking forward to it. I think I've got my muscles in shape again.'

'Oh, good! I'm glad. It looks like being a fine day, too. Though it's misty at the moment it's like that day at Barmouth. The sun will come out and eat it all up and we'll have some splendid views.'

'Any fairies you know about on Helvellyn?' She glanced at him and away mischievously. She was playing with half a grapefruit, and quite literally playing. Not a thing had so far touched her lips.

'No, but there's always the chance. There's magic in mountains, as I think you discovered for yourself. Have a good breakfast. We'll be eating a packed lunch, again, with most of our leg work done.'

'I'm not hungry. I did eat the sandwiches you had sent up to me last night, though.

When do we leave?'

'A little 'bus passes here at nine sharp.'

'Then I'll see you out front at five-to.'

She was up and away in another flash, excusing herself prettily without looking at him.

'Is she dieting or sump'n?' Alf asked of the whole room. 'A little bit of a filly like 'er?'

'I don't know,' Rob said quickly. 'Where are you people going today?'

''Ahnd trails,' said the normally silent Joe. ''Ahnd trails at Grasmere. Watch the dogs work, eh?'

''Sright, mate. 'Ave a little flutter on the side an' a few pints. You look after my gel, nah, Doc. Don't do anyfing I wouldn't do.'

'As you would say, Alf, charnst would be a fine thing!' and to appreciative laughter Rob, too left the dining room.

The little 'bus was narrowly built to cope with the old, winding lakeland roads, and was almost full, when it arrived outside the hotel, of seriously intentioned hikers and climbers. There was a seat for Claire but

Rob stood and pointed out features of interest to her.

'That's Helm Crag. You see the rock formation looks like a man sitting at a piano? Later on, seen from the other side, it's known as the lion and the lamb.'

'I've heard of that,' said Claire. 'My father was a very young curate hereabouts before he married.'

'Once one is up there, on the crag, it's difficult to recognize either of the formations. I scrambled up yesterday, but it was a bit damp, so I soon came down again.'

There was a scraping of heavy nailed boots as the 'bus stopped to allow the serious rock climbers to disembark who were to tackle known faces among the Langdale Pikes. Rob took the opportunity of pointing out a very realistic rock 'lion' to his companion, with a 'lamb' apparently between his great paws.

'It didn't seem very far,' Claire observed as they dismounted a little further on. 'Aren't we cheating using a 'bus?'

'I didn't want to wear you out on the flat,' Rob explained, adjusting the rucksack on his back. 'But we won't be taking the 'bus back. If my geography and maps are correct we should come down behind our hotel eventually.'

They set off up a gentle, rocky slope where others were walking, alone, in pairs or large, laughing groups.

'I couldn't borrow any boots today,' Claire's voice came breathily as she strode out, 'but the hall porter knocked some nails into my brogues. I hope they'll do.'

Rob paused to examine her footwear. She leaned on one of his shoulders and then the other as she lifted her legs in turn.

'I feel like a horse,' she laughed. 'What's the verdict?'

'You should be all right, providing you don't turn an ankle. Just be careful.'

They soon began seriously to climb, although the going was never difficult. Helvellyn is a round, rather than a sheer mountain, but Claire's breathing became laboured and he slowed to observe her.

'You should have eaten breakfast, Claire. Don't you, as a nurse realize that breakfast is the most important meal of the day?'

'Usually. But I have not been my usual self for some time. I have been eating far too much on this trip. Also, as a nurse, I realize that over-indulgence is worse than underfeeding. I'll survive. Carry on!'

Rob occasionally studied a map, took this path, and that, and soon they were alone on a narrow track. He stopped, suddenly, turned her round, kept hold of her shoulders and told her to look.

She almost cried out in the wonder of what she saw. They were surprisingly high up and she could see three separate lakes. One was probably Windermere, long and bright and glistening; another looked deep and lonely with dark peaks frowning into it and yet another was neat and round like a lake in a park. Even further away was a gleam of sea.

'Oh, Rob! Isn't it lovely? It almost makes

me want to cry.'

'Why don't you, Claire? Why don't you cry?'

His hands were still firm on her shoulders and she half turned her head to inquire if he was serious. In doing so she felt his fingers against her neck and for a moment a sweet sensuousness enveloped her. She didn't want to move or the experience to end, and yet its joy was in its brevity, and she knew it. She began to feel like a woman again, a woman with a man after months of living like a nun. It must be stopped before she began to like it too much.

'It *is* very beautiful,' she heard herself say matter-of-factly, and the hands on her shoulders loosened and released her. She thought fixedly about Pete for a moment before turning to continue the climb, but she could now no longer think of Pete without remembering those dreadful innuendoes of yesterday. '–He was the absolute bottom'– 'There was Pete, always chasing girls – sorry, Claire, but he *was* my wayward brother'– 'Didn't Peter leave you properly provided for?' 'Love is very physical at that stage, though, isn't it?' 'Could you be frigid, Claire, to drive my son to drink and to his end?'

A rock went rolling down and fell ker-plump a long way off.

'Well? Do you think you can manage it?' Rob Hirst was asking.

Claire looked at him uncomprehendingly and then shook her head.

'That's OK. We'll go round the long way, then. This is Striding Edge. I was rather thinking you had a head for heights. It's really quite manageable.'

Claire looked at the granite ridge stretching ahead with the ground dropping away quite sharply to the right of it, aware of not having been attending to her where-abouts for some time.

'Of course I'll go on,' she now said clearly. 'I was day-dreaming.'

'Don't daydream for the next fifteen minutes, then, and remember your ankles aren't protected. Simply watch every foothold and keep moving.'

She stepped out after him, aware that she was walking on a narrow ledge almost on the roof of England. Only Skiddaw was higher hereabouts. They had built a bonfire on Skiddaw when the Armada was sighted. Where was Skiddaw from here? 'Could you be frigid, Claire?'– Could she be? *Could* she? She had never allowed Pete to embrace her during parties when he smelled of alcohol; they had never actually been lovers even in these free-for-all days, when most of their contemporaries boasted of their conquests: Claire had determined that only in true marriage would she give herself, and it had been difficult at times when Pete had been so loving and so persuasive. But they had married, and still they had never been lovers. 'Could you be frigid, Claire, to drive my son to drink and to his end?'

She paused to rid herself of the worm eating at the pleasure in the day and found herself swaying, poised on a knife-edge of granite and not recognizing her own scream of sheer terror.

'I – I'm going to fall!'

'No, you're not! No! No! Be still!'

Still she screamed and screamed and screamed even after those strong arms gripped her. The face swam into her consciousness but she couldn't hear the spoken words for the noise in her head.

'I'm sorry about this, Claire,' Rob said quietly, and struck her sharply on the jaw. She collapsed in mid-scream and he gathered her up. When she had first been in his arms, after cutting her leg on the shale, he had felt odd and embarrassed, but now he held her close, in her helplessness, his booted feet firm and sure, and carried her almost joyously along the sharp spur of the Edge to the safety of the sheltered grotto beyond.

Claire had never actually lost consciousness, though Rob had literally knocked her senseless. She rolled her head on the pullover he had placed under it, and opened her eyes experimentally to observe the blue inverted bowl of the early summer sky. She felt in an odd state of hiatus, emotionally, rather as an excited child, promised a treat, will dissolve suddenly into tears. She propped herself up on an elbow and watched Rob busily engaged a few yards away. The rucksack had somehow produced a camping stove and a small frying pan was placed on the burner, from which came a delicious aroma.

'Hello,' greeted Rob, catching her eye. 'Better?'

'Oh, Rob, I'm so ashamed. I can hardly bear to remember.'

'I'm not exactly thrilled about having to strike you, Claire. Does your chin hurt?'

She felt it experimentally, tried stretching her jaw and stood up.

'That's the least of my worries. I was in an absolute, blind panic and deserved all I got. I could have sent both of us crashing down. I – I have never panicked in all my life before, Rob. You must believe me.'

'Then I'm sorry I was the author of it.' He turned thick, speckled Cumberland sausage over in the pan. 'I rather thought you wanted to do the Edge, but if I'd known I wouldn't have allowed you to try.'

She sat opposite him.

'It wasn't the Edge, Rob. I have been rather distraught since yesterday. I thought climbing a mountain might clear my head, but remembering the worst bits in the most difficult places was my undoing. In the circumstances I shouldn't have attempted Striding Edge. I suppose—' she looked intently at the sizzling sausages – 'I value your good opinion of me as a mountaineer, amongst other things, and didn't like to back down.'

He tried not to smile as he thought of her in the rôle of mountaineer on the molehills they had attempted together.

'I wouldn't have thought any the worse of you, Claire, if you *had* backed down. But you didn't, and I admire you for trying with

97

– with things on your mind. Would you like to tell me about yesterday? Only if it would help, I insist.'

'I'd like to tell you. But do you think we could eat? I'm ravenous, now, and smelling that delicious sausage is driving me mad. I thought we were having a packed lunch again?'

'I decided as you hadn't breakfasted we'd have a proper feed. I just have to cook two bantam eggs. The maid at the hotel, who filled my flasks, insisted I take them. When she gave them to me they were still warm.'

As they feasted – and up there where the very air was like wine any meal would have been a feast – she told him of her disillusioning visit to Pete's home and everything which had been said.

'I ended up not only disliking Pete's family but not even sure whether I would still like him if – if he hadn't died. Jane made him sound such a rake, and I remembered how popular he was with certain nurses and even one woman doctor at St Columba's. He would be chatting intently with someone and I would appear and they'd both look self-conscious, and then he would say "Hello, love!" and the other girl would drift away. Maybe he – he wasn't faithful to me. I'll never know.'

'But he married *you*, don't forget.'

'Yes. Maybe the fact that I held out for marriage sent my stock up with him. He used to look at me in a special way, which made me feel I was made out of Dresden china, and I felt precious. I so wanted us to really be together that maybe our haste was a bit indecent, as – as his mother implied.'

'But you were together, finally, and I'm sure he died happy.'

'I may not have made it clear to you, Rob, in my natural agitation, but Pete and I were never together in a marital sense. Sometimes I don't feel married at all.'

'Oh. I think that's very sad.'

'So do I. It may even be that Mrs Matthews is right. I could be frigid, as she says. I mean – how actually does one know? Tell me!'

She was flushed and very lovely in her embarrassed pleading. While her lips were still parted he seized her and pressed his lips to hers with a masculine demand that was at once harsh and revealing. Her faint sounds of protest died as she lost both her breath and her desire to resist. He finally drew away from her but held on to her hands, which he knew were quivering to strike out at him in a natural reflex action.

His eyes on hers were now bold and mischievous.

'I don't know about you, Claire, but I feel a lot better for that. And don't worry, you're not. Frigid, I mean. Now hit me if you still want to,' and he released her hands.

'Oh, Rob!' She stood up and paced about, not caring to remember how on several occasions today she had liked the feel of this man; firstly his hands on her shoulders and the nerve which thrilled in her back to his touch, then that semi-conscious walk when she was pressed close to his heart, which had thundered with the effort, and finally the descent of his lips which had really not come as a surprise. She had played on his masculinity and he had responded; she would have been disappointed if he hadn't, and now she knew that she had liked the experience all too much for her own good. Holiday romances were notoriously ephemeral and she was not an ephemeral person. Where she kissed she gave a little of her heart away, always, and that was dangerous play. Just two weeks ago some girl called Angela had jilted this man – this unknown quantity which was Doctor Robert Hirst – and he could not yet be ready to fall in love again. He had joined her in play; his eyes were still dancing from the experience; and she must respond and restore what was solid about their acquaintance, the friendship. 'Oh, Rob!' she said again, and smiled a little tremulously. 'How absurd! Two adults, who really don't know the first thing about each other, pushed together because they're the two oddments on a package holiday, and playing kissing games on top of a mountain! We're too old for that, surely?'

'We are?' he asked with genuine interest. 'I would say my reactions were exactly right for my age. I was quite satisfied with them. Not,' he added wickedly, 'that I'm used to kissing married ladies. But I think we're agreed you don't come into that category?'

He was busily packing up and had suddenly become an unknown quantity to her by the very fact, it would appear, of getting to know her better. They had not only kissed as a man and woman do, but he had come through as a very dominant male, holding her subject to his will as long as he considered necessary. She had arbitrarily enjoyed being dominated and because he now seemed unaware of her very existence she had a childish desire to irritate him, so as at least to be noticed again.

'You've made my jaw ache,' she grumbled, 'and my dubious tooth is springeing.'

'Let me see.' He examined her teeth with

a scientific rather than a lover-like eye and decided, 'They're perfect. I'm sorry about the jaw. Better an aching jaw than a broken back. I'm ready when you are.'

She trailed after him, still feeling in a pet.

'How is it you know all about me, that you even know my marriage was really only a ceremony, and yet I've learned nothing about *you* apart from the fact that some girl let you down?'

She was sorry the moment she had tossed this at him, for he seemed to grow rigid for a moment before striding on. They were descending by a very easy, roundabout route.

'Thanks for reminding me, Claire,' he said at length. 'I had almost succeeded in forgetting why I'm on an Imperial Tour at all. If I was today nursing any idea that it was to enjoy myself, you have now put me wise.'

'I didn't mean it like that,' she said hastily.

'I think you did,' he snapped. 'I stepped out of line and you decided, in your devious woman's way, to punish me.'

'Oh, no! Oh, no!' She was so eager to deny this that she ran ahead of him and walked backwards as he showed no signs of slowing down.

'I shouldn't do that,' he warned her, 'you should always look where you're going.'

'Then take that back!' she demanded, fiercely, grabbing his arm as he would have pushed past her. He shrugged, however, and she tripped, rolled and fell awkwardly into a little hollow. Her grimace of pain was genuine as she tried to rise. Her right leg remained twisted under her and she sank back, suddenly very pale, so that the bruise on her chin showed startlingly blue.

'What hurts?' Rob asked, leaping down beside her and divesting himself of the rucksack.

'My ankle. Oh!'

'Let me straighten your leg. Hang on to me.'

She drifted almost into a swoon as she felt her brogue unloosed and her sock removed.

A smell of crude ammonia from a small bottle brought her to, however, and she tried to smile reassuringly at her companion.

'Will I live, Doctor?' she asked.

'A sprain. I shouldn't have brought you without boots. I have a bandage which I'll wet from our emergency water bottle. That should ease the pain and keep down the swelling. It may be painful getting your shoe on, again, but we must try.'

When all was done, which could be done, he insisted on giving her a hot, sweet cup of tea from the flask he carried.

'I don't know,' he decided, looking at her much as one would regard a specimen under a slide. She wore a plaster over the cut she had sustained on Cader Idris, and added to her bruised, and decidedly swollen jaw she now had an enlarged, bandaged ankle thrust into her loosely-tied brogue. 'You must be a masochist, Claire, to accompany me anywhere. How am I going to face Alf, eh, with you in this state?'

She looked up at him shyly, wondering if he was still angry, and suddenly they both began to laugh in a way which was almost painful in its relief.

'The uppercut was the worst,' he paused to say, before laughing again. 'I never gave a woman an uppercut before.'

She, too, laughed until she wept. It was some time before they were both sobered enough to converse rationally again.

'There's still the problem of getting you down there,' he said, and cocked his thumb over his shoulder where the mountain track descended. 'You mustn't walk.'

'And there's the problem of what you were saying before this happened,' Claire said. 'I was not intending to punish you for stepping out of line, Rob, though I admit my reference to your past affairs was unkind and uncalled for. There was no line drawn, not by me, beyond which you could not step. As a matter of fact I rather enjoyed what happened, though it may seem immodest of me to admit it. What I've enjoyed of this holiday I've enjoyed because of you. As you've been good for me – and I include the uppercut in that–' at this he smiled a little wryly – 'I would hope I've been good for you, if not equally, then a little. If I appeared to be waspish it was possibly because I was trying to redeem Pete's memory. You seem to know how a woman's mind works and that may make more sense to you than it does to me. I am now concluding, however, that wherever I'm heading it must be forward, and not back. Pete's the past and I've got to go on.'

'I think you're right, Claire,' he told her. 'I can't be the faithful type. I was already concluding the same on my own account.'

'Really?' She searched his face. 'I don't mean, really, aren't you the faithful type, but, really, are you getting over it? You'll meet somebody you'll want to be faithful to eventually, I feel convinced. You're young, very good looking and – and attractive. You'll see.'

'Just imagine!' he said with a wry little

smile. 'Such a recommendation from one who also fits those identical qualities! And so easily we could both go to waste, the way things have happened to us. Hi!' he called, urgently, just as she felt the conversation was becoming interesting, and a group of young walkers approached and – hearing of Claire's 'accident' – volunteered to take it in turns to 'chair' her down the mountain.

Because her ankle remained painful and swollen, and a local doctor advised her to rest it, the next few days were spent, of necessity, merely in travelling in the coach, whither it went, and not leaving the grounds of hotels where the party was deposited. Thus Claire said hello and goodbye to the Scottish seaside resort town of Ayr, not looking at its best in the rain, and to the highlands and Aberdeen, that northern, handsome city of granite, with the weather still lowering and clouds hanging low to obscure what should have been magnificent, panoramic views. By the time the tour had reached Edinburgh, Claire became a bit fretful with her lot.

'You go off and enjoy yourself, Rob,' she commanded rather sharply, as he suggested hiring a car and taking her for a drive. 'What do you want with me hanging about all the time, especially as I am? You're an extremely active person, and you've been very kind in keeping me company these past few days, but I refuse to take advantage of your generosity.'

'I have not considered my motive in staying near you to be generosity,' he said. 'I have enjoyed our games of chess, especially when once you actually out-foxed me and won. My ego took a dip and I wouldn't like to think women were going to make a habit of doing that, I can tell you.' There was a silence between them. 'But, of course, you may want to go on the tour with the others. That would be quite restful for you. I'll mooch around book-shops. There are some very good ones in Edinburgh. I thought I ought to tell you that I'm thinking of leaving for home, tomorrow.'

She tried not to think she had grown quite pale with the shock of his announcement.

'But – but the tour doesn't finish for another four days!' was all she could think of to say in her bewilderment.

'I know. But I didn't come for the tour, Claire. I pushed my unwelcome presence on to our dear Christine to get my breath back after Angela had exploded her bombshell. Thanks to you, in the main, I'm over the worst but I have my future to think of and a great deal to do. I can't really afford four more days of idling at the speed of a 'bus round the country. I can be home by noon tomorrow if I get a fast train.'

'Of course you must do what you want,' Claire said, coolly, and rose from the breakfast table for two they were sharing. She stumbled a little as she reached for the stick which helped her to hobble about and in a flash he had caught hold of her.

'You're angry with me,' he said, quietly.

'I have absolutely no right to be angry

with you,' she spoke without looking at him. 'Good gracious! What a thing to say!'

'I wanted us to have a long chat today. You have accused me of not talking about myself but today I was going to. I felt I needed a friend. Even if a friend can't help they do say a trouble shared is a trouble halved. So how about it, friend?'

She looked up at last with a little smile on her lips and the hurt still in her violet eyes.

'Very well,' she agreed, 'just so long as you're not being your usual charming self by saying all this just to keep me from feeling lonely.'

'I'm not. It keeps me from feeling lonely, too.'

He had hired a self-drive car and they quickly left the city behind and meandered on B roads beside the Firth of Forth, inland, occasionally passing through villages of one-storey houses, so common hereabouts. The sun came out eventually and Rob pulled up in a lay-by beside a little round hill with a magnificent view of the Firth. There was a wrought-iron bench and not another soul in sight.

'Come on!' he invited, and sweeping her up set her down on the bench.

'You are making quite a habit of carrying me,' she decided, 'and I realize I mustn't be content to be – carried by others, I mean. I must learn to stand on my own feet.'

'Morally, you mean? Yes, I agree. But physically you're such a slight little thing it's a real pleasure. I'll bet I could span your waist with one hand.'

She found herself wondering if Angela had been a strapping young woman.

'I'm not thin, you know,' she defensively.

'I do know. During our all-too-brief intimate acquaintance I would say you're nicely rounded in all the right places.'

'Oh.' She found herself blushing and he regarded this phenomenon with interest.

'I didn't mean to embarrass you.'

'Anytime,' she said, and they both laughed, but she became solemn, again, when she realized there wasn't much time left to them. Only what remained of this day.

It was pleasant just chatting and looking down at the shining water, where a tanker was heading out from port into the cold North Sea.

'Let's find somewhere for lunch,' he suggested, eventually. 'I think I know where the very place might be.'

Half an hour's drive brought them to the 'Reeking Lumb'.

'The smoking chimney, to you,' Rob explained. 'The Scots love to fox their Anglo-Saxon visitors.'

There were only two other couples in the dining-room, which was long and low. They ordered thick, home-made Scotch broth, to start with, followed by buttered herrings caught the previous night, soused and baked to a delicious turn. Local raspberries, with cream, seemed ideal for dessert, and when the coffee was served Rob suddenly began to confide.

'I don't know why I suddenly want to tell

you, Claire, of all people but I'm in one hell of a quandary and I've got to do something about it. That's why this lotus-eating expedition has to stop for me. I've got to get back into the real world out there and sort myself out.'

FIVE

Claire listened attentively as he poured out his story. Up to now she hadn't really known much about him, apart from the fact that his love affair had apparently blown up in his face. Now he told her that his father was a County Court judge, and his mother, Lady Margaret, 'fiddled in women's stuff like the Red cross and W.V.S. and helped out on a geriatric ward in the hospital near home.' 'My brother, Tom, took silk and Ben became a solicitor and even my sister Frances, has just finished reading Jurisprudence at Cambridge. I was the family rebel, I suppose, and had other ideas for my future.'

'So you decided on medicine?' Claire prompted.

'Good God! no.' He laughed. 'Have you

been thinking that all the time? Is that why you've used medical terms so confidently in some of our conversations? I don't really know a Potts' fracture from a Colles'. I don't know how Christine got to know about the "Doctor" part; whether I put it on the application form for this tour, in my natural agitation and haste not knowing whether I was on my head or my heels; but I'm one of those dull old dogs, a Doctor of Letters. Robert Nathaniel Hirst, M.A. (Oxon) D. Litt, at your service.'

'I don't think scholars are such old dogs,' Claire said defensively. 'My father was an Oxford man, too, and there was never a dull moment when we were together in the Old Parsonage. What is your subject?'

'I have always had an interest in languages, but gained my doctorate in English literature. I have been tutoring in Oxford very happily. I don't know why I couldn't have been content to go on as I was; I had a very pretty little cottage out at Iffley, but Angela, who had been postgradding, suddenly became disenchanted with the city of dreaming spires. Marriage was to be the open sesame to escape from her studies, which, I learned, were not going too well latterly. She had been advised to start looking for a job with a bank, or the B.B.C., or wherever girls with degrees are employed, and so was planned the supposed marriage of true minds which came to such an untimely end ten days ago. Only ten days–?' he paused to consider. 'Already it seems a lifetime has passed.'

'Hadn't you been in love before?' Claire asked.

'Frequently,' he nodded and smiled. 'In love but not out of this world. I suppose everybody at some time says "This was different". Are you beginning to get the picture?'

'Yes, but I don't see the problem. You have your job, your cottage–'

'Neither. I gave up my job and sold the cottage. I got myself a job at a college in Lucerne. We were going to honeymoon in the Black Forest before I started my duties in September.'

'Then you'll still have *that* job in prospect?' Claire asked.

'Yes. *And* I'm supposed to be a married man by then, remember, and require suitable accommodation? At great pains and expense a furnished flat, overlooking Mount Pilatus, has been procured. Unmarried staff live in the college.'

'So now you either have to tell your new employers that – that you're not getting married after all–?' She looked at him. 'I agree that would be very embarrassing.'

'Or I say I've broken my leg and can't take up my post, or make other excuses; all sounding to me patently like the lies they would be. I made such a fuss about the accommodation when I went for interview, too. Lucerne is not only a popular holiday resort but has a housing problem of its own. I was obviously a popular choice for this post; an Oxford degree still counts for something in this world; and when they found a flat I was told everybody would be most honoured if I would join the staff of the International College, and hoped my dear wife would enjoy her life in Lucerne. I wrote off immediately accepting the post, and I was really looking forward to it. I love Switzerland, and you will already have noticed my affinity with mountains, of which Switzerland has so many glorious examples. For six weeks in Winter the college actually transfers to a village near Grindelwald, and skiing is added to the syllabus of optional subjects. It sounds almost too good to be true, doesn't it? So now I have to get down to thinking what to do. If I'm not going to Lucerne I must tell them very soon, and I must find myself a job. Our family is not wealthy and can't carry dead weight.'

'Still,' Claire said, 'with your qualifications–?'

He grimaced. 'My qualifications, in the present educational climate in this country, are an embarrassment. There are too few jobs, and a great many unemployed teachers. Anyhow, now I've told you I hope you'll understand why I can't waste any more time? No, I don't mean waste, exactly. You have been an oasis in a desert, Claire, and I mean that. I'll remember you long after I've forgotten other things.'

They continued their drive during the afternoon, one or the other occasionally coming up with a suggestion and as quickly turning it down.

'You could go and take up your post,' Claire said at one time, 'settle into the flat, and when somebody mentioned your wife explain that she had been unable to accompany you, maybe owing to sickness in the family.'

They found themselves exchanging uncomfortable glances after a few moments. 'No,' Claire decided, 'I'm not much good at telling lies, either. Whenever I fibbed to my father I would turn bright scarlet, and he always knew.'

'Can you visualize falling in love like that

again?' she asked a little later.

'No. I am determined not to. I shall be totally in charge of my emotions from now on.'

'I can't imagine feeling about anyone as I felt about Pete, either. At the moment I am content simply not to be hurting quite so much.'

'That's a bit negative but I do understand.'

'Have you women friends? And I do mean – friends.'

'Of course. The sort whom one describes as "good chaps". Those who could be one's sisters.'

'Well, I believe many successful marriages are not great romances. People who simply like each other make good partners. Couldn't you think of one such friend who might agree to a sort of platonic marriage? I think most women, no matter how liberated, do enjoy the status of marriage.'

He began to laugh in genuine amusement. 'The woman I like best, in a purely platonic way, would split her tights in derision if I suggested such a liaison between us. Also she is a little older than I am, mentally my peer, and has all the status she needs already. Why don't I put an ad in the paper for an "instant wife"? The replies would afford some entertainment value if the police didn't get to me first.'

'I was only trying to help,' Claire said in a hurt voice.

'I know.' He covered her hand briefly with his own. 'And you have. Anyhow, if that many splendoured thing called love is in the past for you, too, what do you plan on doing with yourself?'

'Like you I have to sort myself out. You said my attitude was negative a little while ago, and I suppose it has been up to now. I have given up my job at St Columba's, I have to go back and sell my home, and on a sudden impulse I told my mother-in-law I was planning to work abroad. That was mainly to let her know I would be out of reach in future. I hadn't seriously considered the possibility.'

'So we're in the same somewhat rocky boat, eh?'

'It looks like it. Only I have made no decisions about my future which have to be either adhered to or undone. Negative again, I suppose.'

It was as though he was thinking aloud.

'My contract is only for a year in the first instance, then renewable for a further three, or not, as things work out. I have no fears about the work side. I'll be dealing with bright youngsters who are being prepared for university entrance. It's akin to taking "A" level students. If I could just face the directors, telling them the truth about Angela crying off at the last minute, kid myself that they weren't feeling sorry for me if I wanted to mooch off on my own, which I will, often...'

'Have they met Angela?'

'No. I merely referred to my fiancée, wife-to-be, that sort of thing. I still wonder why I didn't see it coming; I'm usually quite quick on the uptake and she must have dropped some hint. Ah! she did. I have it now. She said "Let's keep our plans a secret, both from your people and mine, because I've always thought it unlucky to plan too firmly in advance. Things can go agley so easily. Let's make it a *fait accompli* and surprise everybody." Now, why did I just remember that?'

'So your family doesn't know you were planning marriage?' Claire asked.

'No. Nor that I've chucked up my job or applied for another one or that I'll probably be on the dole in about six weeks from now, depending on which way the cat of my impulse jumps. They're in for quite a few surprises one way and another. Well, here we are back in Auld Reekie, and the hire-car men waiting to collect the damages. Thanks for your company,' he said as he helped her out and she tested her weak ankle on the pavement outside the hotel.

'Thanks for the drive,' she responded, as he finished paying the car-hire man and signed the time-sheet required. He offered her his arm which she was glad of.

'You know,' she said confidingly, 'what you really need is somebody like me, at such a loose end that I could spare a year in which to get myself sorted out. I could be your wife-in-name-only, or whichever way you wanted to play it, be your housekeeper and your hostess and you could do the job for which you're so eminently fitted without enduring the embarrassments of humiliating confessions. We could probably have some jolly good times together, climbing mountains with or without a resident fairy and I know I should love learning to ski in Winter. After a year we could review the situation and decide whether or not we wanted to go on, and you could decide about your job at the same time.'

He looked at her in positive amazement.

'And if the decision was to part?' he asked.

'Well, it's your family who are legal eagles. Even I know one can get an annulment for non-consummation of a union, and – and even if there – there has been then people have to live apart for two years, don't they? After all, we've both decided our grand passions are a thing of the past.'

'I suppose you *are* joking?' he asked at length.

The question was never answered for Daisy, who was as thin as her friend, Rosie, was plump was peering anxiously from the head of the stairs.

'Oh, Doctor – Nurse – could you come and look at Alf? He's had a sort of funny turn.'

Claire forgot her weak ankle and sped upstairs with Rob at her heels, entering a bedroom where a shocked-looking Joe kept guard.

'In 'ere,' said Joe, and pointed at the bed where Alf, for once, was not laughing or making jokes. He was breathing jerkily and in obvious pain. He was sweating profusely and looked grey with shock. His skin was cold to the touch.

'Oh, Doc – an' you, Sister Matthews–' said Rosie, tearfully, 'thank God you've come!

The 'otel phoned fer a doctor but nobody's arrived yet. 'E's going ter be orlright, isn't 'e? My Alf? Doc wot do you think?'

'I'm not a Doctor of Medicine, Mrs Twill,' Rob said unhappily. 'But if I can help–?'

'You *can* help, Rob,' Claire said clearly, unbuttoning Alf's vivid-patterned shirt. 'Could you take the pillows away as I lift his head? And give me the eiderdown from the other bed, would you? It's all right, Alf,' she said quietly to the sufferer, who was trying to speak and almost choking with the effort, 'just keep still and you'll be OK. Don't think you're getting out of our date by doing something like this.' All the time she was removing his shoes and then tucking the eiderdown round him.

Rosie was twittering around, crying and saying, ''E 'ad 'an attack like this once before. Not as bad but similar. 'E said 'e felt cold an' 'e was sweating. That's not natural, is it?'

'It happens,' Claire said. 'Now I want you to go and find out if the doctor's coming,

Rosie, because at the moment Alf is better to be absolutely quiet.' To Rob, she said, 'Will you discover what's going on, please? Tell the hotel manager that in my opinion Mr Twill's suffering a coronary thrombosis, and the sooner we get him into intensive care the better.'

'Are you sure, Claire?' Rob whispered, looking rather shocked.

'Well, I've seen plenty in my time and he has all the classic signs. The fact that he's conscious could mean it's a minor artery, but that's for the specialists to say. These early hours in any heart attack are the important ones.'

Within the hour Alf had been taken to hospital and Rosie was allowed to accompany him in the ambulance. Joe and Daisy made their own way to hospital to keep vigil over their friend and a feeling of depression settled over the rest of the company at the hotel so that dinner was a rather dismal occasion. Alf, who had seemed to be such an irritant with his familiarities and jokes to many, at first, had rapidly grown on every member of the party. He was irrepressible and unsquashable and now he was accepted as the joker, with Joe and the two women as straight men, always backing him up and providing the readiest of audiences. Claire, who had been singled out for his particular attentions from the first day was now quite fond of him, and yet she had also suspected the possibility that he was not the picture of brute health he blatantly displayed. He was a typical cardiac-arrest type, in fact, and this was confirmed when Christine addressed them as they sat in the sitting-room awaiting news.

'Well, folks, a message from the hospital about our friend, Alf. He's had a coronary-thrombosis; that is a heart attack; but he's as well as can be expected. I know that's what they always say, but at least he's still alive and I should imagine he's a fighter. They're letting Rosie stay near him and Joe and Daisy are putting up at a hotel near the hospital. They won't be travelling with us tomorrow, but making their way home when Alf's out of danger. Joe says we're not to be miserable or Alf would mind. So, ladies and gentlemen–?'

'We must send him some flowers with all our love and best wishes,' said Miss Durrant. 'Shall we do it collectively or separately?'

'Oh, I think the flowers, collectively, and we can all send get-well cards,' Claire suggested. 'I would like to say that, in my job, I've seen people much worse than Alf get completely better in time. I – I hope he does, anyhow.'

Christine was persuaded to ask George, the driver, to delay the departure from Edinburgh on the morrow for an hour, while flowers and cards were bought and handed in at the hospital and Alf's latest bulletin digested, and while this was being discussed Rob excused himself and left the room.

Claire was brushing her hair, thoughtfully, preparatory to getting into bed when she heard a tap on the door. Some evenings she ordered a cup of cocoa or Horlicks, and had called 'Come in!' before she realized she hadn't ordered anything this time. She was amazed to see Rob.

'Hello!' she was undressed and wearing a wrap so couldn't exactly ask him in.

'Hello, Claire. I've been packing. I've told Christine, but didn't want to make an announcement regarding my planned departure on top of everything else.' Her heart had dropped unaccountably. 'My train leaves very early so I thought I'd say goodbye, now.'

'Goodbye, Rob!' She forced a smile and held out her hand. 'All the very best.'

'And to you. I shall keep check of the Alf situation. The ankle's better, I hope?'

'Much better, thank you. I'd almost forgotten it.'

'I – I saw you in a new light this evening.'

'Oh?' She had been hoping he would leave so that she could indulge in a little weep, but his words intrigued her. 'How?'

'As a capable, ministering little angel. There was I as helpless as a babe, in the situation which confronted us, and you just took over and organized us all and got things done.'

'Well, it *is* my job,' she reminded him.

'That's right. I haven't seen you in the context of your job, of course, and I was impressed. Well, goodbye.'

'Goodbye, Rob.'

He lifted her fingers briefly to his lips, smiled and closed the door after him. She stared at it after he had gone and then sat down weakly on her dressing-stool, staying still for a long, long time.

'Well, that's that,' she decided, eventually, and tossed her head. 'Holiday friendships are notoriously ephemeral. Everybody knows that. We won't give each other a thought after a month or so.'

It was almost exactly a month to the day, a humid day in July, that Claire looked round the living room of Walnut Cottage and

132

decided her first attempts at home decoration were really quite good. She had papered the room and with shades of yellow in the paper and a primrose ceiling, it looked bright and cheerful.

When she had returned from holiday she felt a great sadness engulf her as she opened the front door, and realized this was the sad ghost of herself she had left behind, which must be laid without more ado before it could take permanent root in the place. She had taken Pete's photo out and looked at it, but it was all part of that which was over, a sleeping dog which must be allowed to lie for everyone's good.

She pondered they never got around to decorating the cottage and it was rather gloomy in parts, with beige doors and skirtings.

'I'll decorate the whole place before I put it on the market,' she had decided. 'I'll look in the Nursing Mirror and write off about jobs and decorating will be very therapeutic meanwhile.'

133

Now the main bedroom was a wash of pink and lavenders, and she had bought a new bedspread of pink Nottingham lace.

'I'm mad,' she had decided. 'If I go to New Zealand, or somewhere, I won't be able to take it with me.'

The spare bedroom was colour-washed apple green with pink piping on the doors. The staircase had been difficult, as it twisted, but old Charlie, who looked after the garden, had popped in to give his advice and hold the ladder. Between them they had made a dark-brown staircase white and gleaming, with a thick red-rope hand rail. Encouraged, and again with Charlie's help, she had even tackled some retiling in the kitchen, then painted the cupboards under the sink-unit to match. The old Welsh dresser she had left in its natural oak, just giving it a lick of cedar-oil on Charlie's advice, and with its blue delft it looked cottagey and attractive.

Now the living-room was almost finished and then the whole place would be done.

She just had about a yard of skirting to paint and decided to pause and have a cup of tea, take one out to Charlie, who was mowing the lawn, and then complete her task and think about approaching an estate agent.

While she was handing Charlie his tray of tea and cake she heard the front door bell ring.

'Now who can that be?' she asked, and hurried through the blue-tiled kitchen, regarding it as a would-be house-buyer might, critically, and then into the diminutive hall where she flung open the oak-studded door.

'Oh!' she said, sounding quite shocked, for Rob Hirst stood there, and a very urbane and well-dressed gentleman he looked, in pin-stripes and carrying a bowler-hat and a rolled umbrella.

'You remember me?' he asked, as she still stared.

'Of course I do. Don't be silly! It's just that I'm utterly flabbergasted. Come in!'

'Forgive the city gent look, but I've been

lunching with my father.'

'You look very smart. Oh, my goodness!' she tore a chequered scarf off her head, suddenly aware of the old paint-splashed jeans she was wearing. She had a dab of yellow paint on her nose. 'I'm decorating,' she told him, 'but I was just stopping for tea. Will you join me?'

'I'd love a cup of tea. What a very pretty cottage!'

'You think so? I'm waiting to sell it so I thought I'd do it up. Probably the new people won't approve my taste but it has been quite enjoyable. Will you go into the living-room?'

'Why not the kitchen? I'm sure that's where the tea is. I am a kitchen person, myself.'

'Come on, then.'

She took two china cups from the dresser and began to pour.

'Have you heard about our friend Alf?'

'Not for a week. They'd transferred him to Battersea General when I last asked.'

'Well, now he's home and has been told if he behaves himself he should return to normal in about another eight weeks. He was quite cocky when I called, and sent you his love. He was surprised that we were no longer in touch, you and I. Apparently it was commonly supposed that we had "something going" between us on the tour.'

She smiled over her cup, a little shyly and watchfully. Surely he hadn't called just to reassure her about Alf?

'You're not far from the M40, here,' he decided, 'so I should be back in Oxford within the hour.'

'So you're still at Oxford?' she asked politely.

'I have rooms in College until the end of the month. It's the long vac, as you know, but I've had a couple of summer-school student bodies in residence since I saw you last. So I am not still at Oxford as I think you mean it, Mrs Matthews. I have to get out soon. There's one more official function for me, a Graduation Ceremony. That's what I came to see you about.'

'Oh. Why am I Mrs Matthews, suddenly?'

'Because I don't wish to presume on our very brief acquaintance. By the way, what's up with your 'phone? I've been trying all week to get you. I thought you might have considered my dropping in, without warning, a confounded cheek.'

'Oh! The 'phone's a bane. The engineers keep coming and it goes for a few days, then it breaks down again. They tell me the installation's very old and the underground cable may need to be renewed. As there's a public call-box at the end of the lane I haven't bothered. If anybody wants to call me, of course, it is very awkward. What exactly is a Graduation Ceremony?'

'Oh, it's quite charming, really. The Vice Chancellor presents the new graduates with their diplomas and everybody is robed and gowned. It hasn't changed since Chaucer's day and the whole business is conducted in Latin. If that sounds dull the spectacle and the ceremony make up for it. Broad Street will be thick with American tourists plus ciné cameras, who love our traditions. I wondered if you would care to attend as my guest…?'

'Well…' she drew a programme he offered her closer and read, without really seeing, 'Summer Graduation, Sheldonian Theatre, Oxford'. 'Why ask me?' she wanted to know. 'Not to say goodbye again? I hate goodbyes.'

'No, it's not to say goodbye again. We could do that, now, with a simple cheerio. I only want you to attend the ceremony as my guest on one condition.'

'Oh?' she queried, and shrugged. 'I simply don't follow.'

'Do you remember our day in Edinburgh when we drove around discussing my problems, in the main, and yours to a lesser extent?'

'I do, yes. I remember it in part.'

'Well, just before we heard of Alf's collapse, do you remember making a suggestion to me which was so utterly audacious I couldn't believe my ears?'

She thought and then blushed crimson.

'Yes, I do,' she admitted. 'It was audacious and I apologize. I don't think I really knew what I was saying. A jumble of words just bubbled up inside me almost of their own volition. Don't give the matter another thought.'

'I have thought of nothing else since,' he now told her. 'When those suggestions came bubbling up of their own volition you became the picture of vivacity. It was the first time I had seen you sparkling like champagne since we met. It was a serious little face I beheld for so long, not sad, but wearing a mask of mute acceptance that life was not exactly a bed of roses. Even when you smiled it was always just with your mouth. Your eyes were bruised violets. At least, that is how I thought of them. Then, suddenly, on that day, you were charged with exhilaration, as though what you said excited and thrilled you. You made the idea of our life together in partnership sound like a challenging adventure. I am not one to resist a challenge I, too, find attractive. As I remarked, I have given a lot of thought to what you said, and you have obviously only just remembered it. You may have made plans for your future already, and if so I hope God goes with you. If not, perhaps you would like to think of us as a partnership much on the lines you spoke of. First thoughts are quite often the best thoughts by their very spontaneity. I don't want you to say anything just now, because I have obviously shocked you by speaking of such things, but only come to the Graduation Ceremony if you are prepared to discuss things further. You will still not irrevocably commit yourself by such discussion. I am intending taking up my post in Lucerne whatever happens, so don't think that your decision will affect my immediate future professionally. It could add considerable zest to it, I am prepared to say. I am even prepared to say I like you as a person, and as a woman enough to share my life with you. Now I'm leaving and I hope a saucepan doesn't follow in my wake, as a sign of your immediate reaction to my proposition. It could well damage that beautifully painted door. On the programme is the number of the seat you will occupy if you turn up at the ceremony. I hope you will, but – feel free. Good afternoon, Claire. Thanks for the tea. You have a spot of paint on your nose. It quite becomes you.'

As the door closed after him, a burning sensation, which had started in her stomach, seemed to rise and almost choke her as it finished in her blazing eyes. She rushed to the hall window to behold a white Jaguar pulling away from her front gate with Charlie leaning on the mower looking after it.

'Fancy him remembering a thing like that!' she found relief in almost shouting. 'Just who does he think he is? God's gift to women? He must have realized I was only joking. Surely he's not serious in imagining we could make a go of it? A – a marriage without love? Doing all the things married

142

people do as a sort of exercise?' She went back to her unfinished painting and lashed away savagely with her brush, leaving more splashes to be cleaned up than ever before. 'And yet,' she pondered, 'wasn't it I who said that not all married people were passionate lovers? That people who simply liked each other often made very good partners?'

The work she had been loth to finish was now completed and dismissed from her mind within half an hour. She felt, instead of being once more in a state of hiatus, that she suddenly had a great deal to think about.

SIX

Claire became quite annoyed with the senior of the two telephone engineers who had once again arrived to see to her 'trouble'.

'Look!' she said, her eyes flashing, 'I receive my bills, I pay my rental and I'm getting hardly any use out of my damned 'phone. Find what the trouble is and fix it. That's your job.'

'Look, lady, Mm–'

'I don't want to look at anything or listen to excuses. The underground cable is your affair, not mine. When my 'phone's working there'll be a pot of tea for you.'

The engineer looked after her and winked at his mate.

'What made me think she wouldn't say boo to a goose, that one, eh, Bill? A proper little fire cracker she is today. Well, let's get on. Dig a few 'oles for starters, shall we?'

It was two days since Rob Hirst's surprise call and now Claire had more or less remembered every word she had said to Rob on that day in Edinburgh, and remembering had brought back other things. She could recapture the smell of his thick, fair hair, dampened with rain, and sense the feel of his hand under her elbow when she had 'gone lame', and leant on him more heavily than she had needed to, she had to admit. His countenance smiled ruefully at her from corners, or blazed at her icily, as in that moment before he had knocked her out on Striding Edge. He was filling the cottage without being in it, so that Pete was now totally consigned to memory. She could remember his arms reaching for her and the gentle, firm investigation of his lips on her own. A kiss being said to be as individual as a finger-print, she could only remember the breathlessness of her reaction and that he had withdrawn before she was quite ready to put a label on the event.

She said 'Damn the man!' a dozen or more times a day and riffled through the programme of the Graduation Ceremony until it began to look like last week's newspaper. Clumsily she translated the latin text from her remembrance of 'O' level and her father's latin dictionary.

'Anybody would think I was considering going,' she had said at one point and then paused to ask herself if she was.

'Oh, damn that telephone!' she had moaned at one point, because it would have been so easy to pick up the 'phone and tell Doctor Robert Hirst of twenty reasons why she would not be seeing him again. Hence the presence of the green van outside her door, on this occasion, and the sight of a tin-hatted engineer disappearing down a hole. She was also aware of the fact that *he* still could not 'phone *her* if he felt like it, whereas she simply had to walk down the lane to delivery her sharp, succinct and out-raged response to his immoral suggestion.

The senior engineer came smiling to the back door eventually.

'Try it now, Mm,' he invited. 'Go on! try it. Ring the G.P.O.'

She did so and an operator told her to replace the receiver and she would be rung back. The bell shrilled a moment later.

'Good!' she said. 'I appear to be working again. Thank you.'

'But for how long this time?' she asked big Harry, whom she was getting to know by now.

'Oh, I think you'll find your troubles are over, love. We've laid a temporary cable under your hedge. It shouldn't bother anybody there. You can ring the boy friend now, eh?'

'I promised you a drink,' Claire said levelly, 'but it doesn't have to be tea. It's a hot day and I have some cans of beer.'

'Now you're talking,' said big Harry, accepting two cans of beer, sweating from the fridge, but refusing glasses. 'Thank you, lady. Glad to oblige.'

With the Graduation Ceremony on the following Tuesday, and neither having 'phoned Rob nor heard from him, on the Saturday Claire hied her into London with a view to buying a nice little suit, or something, not for any specific occasion but just in case.

'If I do decide to go I want to look good when I tell him he was mad to think I would consider such an alliance,' she told herself in the train. 'Simply not turning up isn't my idea of settling anything. As *he* would say, it's too negative.'

She decided on a dark blue denim suit, with white decorative stitching. It looked young and cool, and she had never been what she called a 'frilly' type. With a couple of polka dotted blouses she felt satisfied with her purchases and went back home quite early to relax with the 'Telegraph' crossword puzzle. But somehow she couldn't concentrate. Even looking round at her newly decorated rooms unsettled her; she saw a 'bubble' under the paper here, brushmarks on the paintwork there.

'So what?' she asked herself. 'If the people who buy the cottage don't like it they can do it all over again. I've got to get all this trivia out of my mind and really start living again.'

She had a trunkful of her father's papers, sermons, letters, travel brochures and the like. She now rushed upstairs and pulled down the ladder which led into the loft. There was a light up there and now she switched it on, opened the trunk, shrank a little as a large spider emerged, appeared to regard her with beady eyes out on stalks, then slid over the edge and scampered away. She then ferreted until she found the old brochures. As a young, penurious student and – later – a curate, John Trent had taken the Youth Hostel trails all over Britain and Europe, living frugally, walking in the main and sleeping eight to a room in hostels wherever they might be. Therefore it was to be expected that the brochures he had left favoured hikers, the maps showed clearly marked footpaths, usually overlain with a red pen where he had actually travelled, and noted in the margins labelling hostels as good!! bad! rotten!! awful food!!!! and the like.

Claire lovingly straightened out the large map of Switzerland and sought out the lake and city of Lucerne, which was spelled Luzern on the map. Her father had written an excellent!! for one hostel overlooking the lake, and noted that one couldn't go wrong for a walking holiday in that vicinity. The Lake of Geneva was lacking in comment so her father had obviously not been there, but the Bernese Oberland was stabbed and starred with red, and great exclamation marks filled the margin. 'I felt so close to God here,' he had written at one point.

Claire folded up the map. It was like her father's soul still crying out and was peculiarly private. She was not even considering going out to Switzerland to find God, but – if she did so decide – to live with a man she did not really know at all, and yet whose unkind fate had nudged against her own for a brief while in a kind of intimacy. Already she was aware of the fragility of holiday friendships; the man in the city suit, who had surprised her by calling and taking tea with her, before reminding her of a wild proposition she had made, was not the same creature who had practically dragged her up a Welsh mountain and told her a fairy story; he was not the same person who had met her off the train after that disastrous meeting with her in-laws, exuding strength and comfort and asking nothing in return, not even her confidence; he was not the jilted and offended lover bolting blindly for the anonymity of a heterogeneous party of coach-trippers. He had been the true Robert Hirst, and a person she didn't really know at all and yet about whom she had to admit to a gnawing curiosity.

'That's enough for now!' she told the empty attic, bundling back the papers she had disturbed before asking, less confidently, 'Do you want to go back, too, spider?'

She crept down the ladder, surveyed the dust on her person ruefully and made a beeline for the bathroom.

'I'm not going,' she decided that night as she brushed her hair. 'I'm surprised I'm still even remotely entertaining the idea.'

On Tuesday morning, a day so hot and humid that she even carried the denim jacket over her arm, she was on a train bound for Oxford, that city of dreaming spires or lost causes, depending upon one's mood. Claire's mood was locked in the butterflies which disturbed her stomach. She was going to see him again. The final goodbyes had still not been said.

Claire had visited Oxford only once with her father, when she had taken tea with him at Queen's, his old college. She remembered it as a city thick with bicycles, and cool pools of green lawns seen behind oak-studded gate-house doors. Now it was the long vacation, however, and only a few students were in residence, maybe for extracurricular studies or because they had nowhere else to go. The city was athrong, however, with sightseers pouring in and out of the old colleges in the wake of couriers: there were the young of continental Europe, too, with all but the kitchen stove on their strong young backs. The Graduation Ceremony was at twelve and members of the public were asked to be in their seats by eleven-thirty. There was more than the usual flurry, therefore, outside the Sheldonian Theatre in Broad Street. Rumour that something was happening had spread like wild fire and police were asking crowds to move along without much success. There were even coaches, on tour, pausing to catch anything of what might be going on and causing great traffic congestion in the already fully parked street.

Claire showed her programme to an usher who personally guided her to her seat up in the gallery. The theatre was magnificent, round in shape and with beautiful carvings everywhere; a domed ceiling which would not have shamed a medieval cathedral chapel. People were crowding in, filling up the seating to capacity, no doubt most of them proud parents come to watch their sons and daughters crown their careers by receiving the degrees for which they had worked so hard. The students began to arrive in the theatre with their tutors, and were shepherded to their seats on the ground floor, the girls wearing black skirts, white blouses with little black ties and Chaucerian caps and gowns; the boys in dark suits with black ties on their white shirts, and also shrugged into gowns. Their headgear was the mortarboard. Claire was amazed at the youthful appearance of the graduates, who must, on average, be aged twenty-one. She was only twenty-four herself, and yet managed to feel like one of the adoring aunts they had brought along. Three years older, she thought ruefully, and such a world of experience dividing her from them.

Suddenly she recognized Rob Hirst. His

countenance was stern and his eyes watchfully on the thirty or so young men he
accompanied. To her they seemed that
much better scrubbed and more carefully
attired than the others. Not a tie-knot was
awry, and the only bearded member was
carefully trimmed into neatness. Robert,
himself, wore a mortarboard and a scarlet-
lined hood over his gown. She fancied he
glanced up and her hand was half-raised to
salute him when he looked past her and all
around the gallery. She knew that he knew
she was there but was not prepared to make
a song and dance about it. What was happening to him, in that knowledge, she didn't
know, but her own heart was racing. She
rose automatically as the Vice-Chancellor
and other Members of Congregation
entered and sat at a high table. An official
began to pound with a staff and intone, and
two velvet-sleeved Proctors walked up and
down the rows of students, carrying out a
time-long function of seeming to be looking
for intruders or undesirable visitors in the

ranks of the learned.

Firstly there was applause as the great doors opened facing the high table and a phalanx of older students marched in to be given their Masterships. Each one individually shook the Vice-Chancellor's hand and went out by a side door with the new dignity of adding M.A. (Oxon) after his or her name. The new B.A's were not given the personal treatment. They were paraded in scores, with their tutors, with the advance guard exchanging bows with the great ones on behalf of the rest. With the latin intonations, and the graduates' replies, and the Proctors marching up and down, up and down, Claire lost track of Rob and then she heard his voice. In impeccable latin he was presenting his students to the Vice-Chancellor.

Claire's heart swelled with pride for him. He appeared to have more graduates than anyone else, but she had to admit that maybe English was a popular subject. Still–

Cameras were flashing all over the theatre

and it seemed that too soon the Vice-Chancellor's procession was leaving and the ceremony was over. Out in the quadrangle there were hundreds of photographic sessions going on, as the new B.A's and B.Scs were 'snapped' by their relatives and friends in their hired finery. Pressed to the railings were the tourists, firing ciné cameras at all and sundry. Rob's hand rested under her elbow momentarily.

'Hello! I'll be two minutes getting this lot off. Don't move or I'll lose you.'

'Rob?' now a girl's hand was on *his* arm. She was tall and fair with a tip-tilted nose. 'How are you?'

'Good afternoon! Very well, thank you,' and he turned and strode away.

'Hello!' the girl greeted Claire. 'Have we met? Were you at Oxford?'

'No. No, I wasn't.'

'Oh. Well, I'll push off. Hot, isn't it?'

Claire tried not to think the atmosphere had suddenly cooled, however, and she was convinced of it when Rob rejoined her and propelled her through the crowd, down a couple of side streets and to the white XJ6 Jaguar she had seen before.

He handed her into the passenger seat and was soon sitting beside her, feeling for his car keys in his dark suit pocket.

'Was it tiring for you?' she asked politely.

'Not at all. One gets used to such things.'

'You look odd. Are you ill?'

'No, I'm not ill.'

'I'm glad.'

But she was aware that the dark side of him she didn't know was in control of him at this moment. She almost imagined he had forgotten her existence as he made rude remarks about a car reeling drunkenly round and round a round-about. The silent car deceptively topped the fifty mile an hour limit without appearing to do so and suddenly the country was very flat and one could believe the story that the City of Oxford was built on a reclaimed marsh.

'Wolvercote,' she said, as they passed a village sign.

'Yes. We're lunching at the Trout,' he told her, turning right off a suicidally narrow little lane into a parking lot. 'We should get to our table before the rabble arrives.'

She exclaimed in delight over the old inn, where a bustling little river ran through its back garden with a weir and fish jumping for joy in the tumbling water which a broken wooden bridge spanned.

'Do you want a drink first?' he asked, she fancied impatiently.

'No. We'll eat. Before the rabble arrives, I think you said?'

He gave her an assessing look as they were shown to a table for two in an alcove.

'Why the cynicism?' he asked her. 'Any special reason for it?'

'No. Nothing has happened to upset *me*.'

'Meaning–?'

'Well, obviously *you* are upset. You're like a thundercloud, suddenly. It was Angela, wasn't it?'

'What about Angela?'

'That was Angela who came and said hello.'

'Did you have a girlish chat together?'

'No. But as she's been rearing between us ever since it might be as well to talk about her. She – she's very pretty.'

'I don't doubt but that she would agree with you.'

'Maybe she wants to make things up between you. Have you considered that?'

'I don't want to talk about Angela, if you don't mind. We met today, you and I, to talk about us. I don't suppose my behaviour has argued exactly in my favour, but I don't want to give the impression that I have gone off the notion of our marriage of convenience. May I recommend the steak? It's really grilled to a turn, here.'

Claire nodded to the waitress who was hovering over them and then began to laugh uninhibitedly.

'I can't help it,' she told him in explanation. 'The whole thing's so absurd that I came to tell you you had a damned cheek even to think I meant a word of what I said on the spur of that foolish moment in

Edinburgh. But the subject just refuses to be buried. It's like an acorn that has put down a root or two, and before you know where you are is a tree. Now how could you consider such a plan? I've seen Angela, now, and I realize how deep the feeling must have been between you. She's attractive, and – she may, really, have discovered her mistake by the odium of comparison. She obviously wants to see *you* again.'

'Why do you insist on digressing? We either talk about us, as a team, or we forget it, finish our meal and go our ways. I would, personally, rather go along with you.'

'But – but you really don't know me. You can't.'

'I would enjoy the opportunity of learning about you. I should find the subject fascinating.'

She felt herself flushing as he examined her features.

'I – I may snore or – or leave wet towels on the bathroom floor,' she stammered.

'So? On the first count I would pinch your

nose and on the second I would insist on you picking them up.'

She gave an uncertain little smile. 'We're being ridiculous, you know. If it's a woman you want you don't have to marry her.'

'If you are the woman I want would you settle for a liaison outside of marriage?'

'No. But I'm an old-fashioned sort of girl.'

'I happen to like old-fashioned girls in that respect.'

The steak arrived at that moment and gave them respite. The fillets were thick and rare with browned onions and tiny mushrooms mixed in the peas in an accompanying dish.

'Can you cook?' Rob asked.

'I think I'm pretty fair. I'm rather good with pastas. My cakes go sad in the middle.'

'I'm not much of a cake man. More for the cheese. Now, anything else to be discussed?'

'Oh, Rob, you are absolutely impossible!'

He looked at her and her countenance held that light again, as though it was lit within with the soul's radiance.

They ate the main course with real enjoyment, accompanied by a warm dark Burgundy. As she said 'Thank you. That was gorgeous!' he reached out and took her hand so that she raised her eyes to his and lingered a fraction too long for her own comfort. The exchange of glances became intense, meaningful.

'Sir? Sorry to butt in. But could I introduce my parents?' A shining young man stood there with a couple hovering behind him. 'Awfully sorry, sir, to interrupt but we can't find a table. I didn't book in advance.'

'Have ours,' Robert invited, shaking hands dutifully with the parents. 'We're just going to have some ice-cream outside. I'm sure they'll find you another chair. Got a job yet, Nigel?'

'Practically, sir. I'm on two short lists.'

'Well, good luck!' He drew Claire after him and towed her out into the garden where he looked hard at a couple of students until they vacated the table they were sharing over beers.

The waitress Rob seemed to know came out with ices and coffee and they continued that somewhat dangerous conversation at greater leisure.

'Well,' he decided a length, 'so far you haven't shot me down in flames. I presume we are still discussing the possibility of our marriage? If not we certainly should be, because the ceremony would be here a week from today. I have the necessary residential qualifications at present.'

'A week today? A *week?*' she looked stunned. 'Oh, Rob, how could you expect–?'

'Because havering always makes decisions more difficult. It is best to say yes, and get on with it, or no and keep to it.'

'I don't think you've begun to think of the difficulties. I sometimes think we're not speaking of the same thing.'

'We're discussing marriage. How much clearer can I make that?'

'Yes,' she said, spiritedly, 'marriage and all that it implies. Being tied to each other, legally, and – and me having to change my name again. That would be twice within a year. Have you thought of that?'

'I want us to think of such things. That's why we're here. You don't fancy being Claire Hirst, then?'

'What's in a name?' she asked impatiently. 'It's the status that counts. For instance, what do we do about the – the emotional side of things? Do we live together in – in every sense of the word?'

'Well, do we?'

'You see? You leave all the major decisions to me.'

'Only because I think you should direct me so that I know you feel comfortable about things. If you say you don't want to sleep with me, then I'll respect your decision.'

'No! no!' she said quickly. 'I don't say that at all. To put a veto on the most natural of instincts would be to give it an unhealthy importance. I think we should wait and let happen what will, when we're both a bit better acquainted. I – I would never lock my husband away from me. That would be setting out on the wrong foot from the start. Of course I'm not saying I'm going along with this lunatic plan, it's just that as a piece of pure fiction I still like things to be tidy.'

He again placed a hand over hers and she tried not to meet his eyes this time.

'As a piece of pure fiction could we even suggest we might manage to live happily ever after?' he wanted to know.

'One can manipulate the characters in books, but real people are a different kettle of fish.'

'I shall not refrain from saying that your simile stinks.'

She looked at him this time and her smile was tremulous and uncertain.

'You don't hate me, do you, Claire?'

'Of course I don't hate you. I like you. But I don't really know enough about you.'

'I can produce a history sheet within the hour and several references.'

'Fool.'

'If you don't marry me, tell me what your alternative plans are.'

'I had a letter this morning inviting me to go along for interview to a private clinic in Jersey. I would be in full charge.'

'So young to be so responsible. That's what you want to do, is it?'

She looked at the tumbling river and the old, broken bridge and could visualize herself in a plain dress with lace collar and lace Matron's cap in the antiseptic atmosphere of a clinic where the well-to-do came to have their operations and – perhaps – their abortions.

'I was rather thrilled by the idea this morning,' she had to admit. 'Now I'm not so sure.'

'Why not?'

'Because I've had this extremely disturbing meeting with you and nursing in Jersey seems dull compared.'

'You mean you really would consider–?'

She made up her mind at that moment.

'Yes, Rob, I'll marry you. Go ahead and

make the arrangements. I only hope I can make you happy, but if I don't – or either of us is dissatisfied in any way – after a year we'll say goodbye with dignity. I trust.'

'Good girl!' he told her. 'Who was it said women were over-emotional to make up for their lack of mind?'

'You said a week today?'

'I did. Is that all right with you?'

'I haven't even put the cottage on the market, yet.'

'Don't worry. After the ceremony you can go back home and see to such things. I have a lot to see to, also, so I may have to neglect you for a week or two. When you're my beautiful bride you'll need your passport changing.'

'What – what about my wedding ring?'

She was turning the thin gold band round and round in her nervous excitement.

'Wear it on a locket or have a stone set in it. I would rather like to buy you a new one.'

'Very well. Is – is that all, then?' She stood up and looked at her watch, amazed that it was almost four p.m.

'I don't think we've even begun but I'm sure we both need time for reflection. Do you think – I mean is there even a possibility that you'll change your mind?' She saw the darkness behind the vivid blue of his eyes and remembered him as he had first stalked down the 'bus in Victoria Coach Station.

'No. That's what I've been doing all afternoon. Now it's made up. You needn't worry that I – I won't be there. I had better add providing I haven't broken my back or something equally disabling.'

'Please don't ever break your back, Claire. Oh! Any other names besides Claire?'

'Elizabeth, my mother's name.'

'And there are two T's in Matthews?'

'Yes.'

As they drove back towards Oxford she saw it much as Jude must have seen it, a kind of silver grey silhouette in a wash of heat-haze.

'It's been a quite amazing day,' she concluded, as they waited for the London train coming in. 'I think I'd better go in a non-smoker as I suddenly feel faint.'

'Claire?' he was staring at her anxiously, and she really did look pale.

'Oh, I'm all right. Nurses have to be as strong as oxen. But I suppose even nurses can suffer from shock.'

'Would you like me to see you home?'

'No. Of course not.' The train came in and he saw her to a carriage, still looking anxious.

'It's all the wine,' she concluded. 'I'm not used to it. We must have drunk four bottles. Do get off or you'll be too late.'

He stooped and kissed her, much to her surprise, and then darted off the train with nimbleness she hadn't suspected in him. She watched him until the platform gave out and then realization washed over her and she really did feel faint as she put her face forward into her hands.

'Oh, dear God!' was torn from her. 'I do hope I'm up to all I've promised him and I'll try, I really will try to make it happy ever after.' It was true of the girl she was that it was Rob Hirst who came foremost in her thoughts now that she had promised herself to him. The happiness she found for herself would be purely coincidental.

She put her hand to her lips where his kiss still burned and suddenly she was tingling all over.

'I said I wouldn't shut him out, and I won't,' she decided. 'The very idea of such a thing, as though we were two children!' She watched the lush meadows rushing by. 'But I know when he does come I – I'm going to be very, very nervous,' she now admitted. 'After all, I still hardly know him. It's just that I like him and I've promised to marry him.'

She simply daren't trust her thoughts any more after that.

SEVEN

Claire awoke in the Oxford hotel where she had booked in the previous evening, and watched, on her wedding day, the rain sheeting down as it often can do when the weather breaks after a hot spell, with an almost tropical density. She felt odd, as she had all the past week, as though she did everything mechanically while her emotions were locked securely away where they couldn't be harmed.

Therefore even the rain did not dismay her particularly; she felt it rather fitted the occasion; two people who were not in love were getting married in a Register Office at eleven-fifteen precisely.

'Don't be late,' Rob had requested when he had informed her of the time and the venue over the 'phone, 'apparently the

Registrar does this every fifteen minutes.'

'Then I must stay in Oxford the previous night,' Claire had responded, 'otherwise it would be an awful rush. Could you suggest a hotel where I might get in?'

'I'll see to that. The Rosery on the Headington Road. I know the proprietors. Shall I call and see you settled in?'

'No. There's no need for that. You'll have things to do as I will. If that's all, I have some people coming to look over the cottage.'

'Yes. That's all. Good luck with your prospective buyers, but hold out for your price. See you, then.'

'Yes. See you.'

Now she turned away from the window and winced from the breakfast tray by her bed. She felt peculiarly sickened by the sight of food.

'Well, at least I know I'm not pregnant, nor likely to be,' she concluded wryly, as she emptied the coffee jug down the wash-basin and crumbed a slice of toast to place on the tiny balcony outside the window for the birds. She stirred up the marmalade so that it looked as though she had taken some, then put the tray outside the door.

She showered and began to dress. When she had finished, apart from her hair, which still hung loose, she regarded herself in the long, wardrobe mirror.

'It's either distorted or I've lost weight,' she concluded, running her hands over the white-silk jersey of her clinging dress. 'I look like a bean-pole.'

But really she looked fresh and sweet, dainty and slim; the heels of her white court shoes made her appear taller than usual. Only her countenance was somehow blank, as though she had ceased to live in it.

Mechanically and deftly she dressed her hair, softly over her ears and neatly in a fold behind.

There was a tap on the door.

'Yes?' she called out. Surely it wasn't the taxi already? A wave of blind panic engulfed her.

'For you, Madam,' the maid was holding a spray of yellow roses in the usual plastic packing. 'Would you like me to put them in a vase?'

'Thank you. Yes, please.' She opened the envelope the girl handed to her. There was a verse of poetry written on the card but no name, yet only one other person knew she was here.

'I think of you as of an April day,
 Which through the rain gives promise
  of the sun,
 And frets the while her dancing glances
  play,
 And weeps from eyes that late a smile
  begun:
Your eyes smile with a hint of ready pain,
As April's shine with rain.'

'Oh!' Claire exclaimed in pleased surprise, and, seated as she still was at the dressing table, looked in the mirror to behold her countenance suddenly glowing and – as the poem said – her eyes threatening an imminent April shower. 'Oh! How nice! I think that's the first time I've had poetry quoted at me, and it's very touching. I wonder if he does think of me like that?'

The girl returned with the yellow roses pouring out their scent and bringing the sun with them. Yes, it had stopped raining and now the sun was brilliant and the sky herring-boned to the horizon.

Quite jauntily, now, Claire made up lightly; a little eye-shadow, a touch of lip-stick. Her eyelashes were naturally long and dark, and curled gently. She pulled a little white pill-box hat over her hair and then, on impulse, cut two of the roses short with her nail scissors and, making a nest of the accompanying maidenhair fern for them, pinned them to her dress, just above her heart.

The taxi should be arriving at any moment so she must hurry. Through the thrills of excitement shooting through her she felt an odd twinge of pain as she removed Pete's ring from her left hand, and again thought how apt the poem was. She was a shine and shower person on a shine and shower day.

The telephone by her bed rang and she was informed a car was awaiting her. Picking up a small white pouch bag she went downstairs resolutely and instructed the driver to take her to the Register Office.

Her memory seemed to blank for a while after that and she came back to full consciousness to find herself standing beside the almost total stranger who was becoming her husband. The tall, handsome, well-tonsured man in grey, with the white carnation in his buttonhole, the silver-grey tie beautifully knotted, was as utterly unknown to her as any stranger in the city. It seemed that Rob had only to change his clothes to appear to her like a chameleon, utterly unrecognizable. She hadn't noticed until that moment of meeting on the steps of the Register Office just how good-looking he was. He was Viking blond with eyes the colour of periwinkles. He looked slim in the well-cut suit, but she knew the breadth of his shoulders and the power in the arms that had lifted her up like a kitten on more than one occasion. While she was trying to smile at him she saw him not alone, but accompanied by a tall, slim, blond young boy, as his son would one day look. Shaking her head the boy slid away as a vision and all the confusion began. She was being helped up into the building and a clock, with a dark, brown chime, struck the quarter after eleven. They had no witnesses. The couple who had married at eleven o'clock laughingly consented to act, sharing intimate glances and secret jokes.

'I have to know your date of birth, Mrs Matthews,' the Registrar was saying for the second time. 'It *is* Mrs Matthews?'

'Sorry,' somebody else said out of her mouth. She told the official she was born on the second of January, and the year.

'Now–' said the Registrar, and the cool, legal and yet meaningful ceremony was somehow accomplished. There was even a little homily to follow. The man, who was possibly in his middle forties, advised them to take their partnership seriously, to be willing to give and take and never to allow the sun to go down on their wrath.

'I know you'll think me mad to speak of rows on your wedding day, but you'll have them. We all do.'

'I intend to beat my wife every Friday night, regularly,' Rob suddenly said ringingly, making her jump to attention, 'and twice on Sundays.'

The Registrar looked dubiously up at the other and back to Claire, then raised eloquent eyebrows and shrugged.

'Very well,' he said, 'good luck.' With scarcely a pause he addressed his clerk. 'Next, please.'

'So that's that,' Rob said, out in the street again. 'Quite painless, wasn't it? Come on! We do look a bit dressed up for the public gaze.'

She couldn't yet link events together but found herself in the dim saloon bar of an exclusive pub with a glass of champagne in front of her.

'Now let's have a proper look at you,' Rob said, pulling her to her feet. 'I got the impression when I first saw you that you were doing me proud, and so you are. And in white, too!'

'That wasn't meant to be significant,' Claire said. 'I saw the dress, liked it, and it just happened to be white. I would probably have bought the same dress had it been blue. By the way, thanks for the roses and poem. Who wrote it?'

'Old Anon. It's called "Six Lines",'

'He wrote a lot, didn't he?' she smiled up at him suddenly, again with that April change of mood. 'You look very nice, too.'

'Thanks!' he said, filling up her glass recklessly so that it frothed over. 'For turning up on time and everything.'

'I said I would.'

'I hope you didn't think me frivolous shutting up that pompous ass. "Don't let the sun go down upon your wrath," indeed!

He made me feel sixteen.'

'I'm sure he meant well,' Claire decided. 'The look he gave me was very understanding and sympathetic. When you do decide to beat me, by the way, I must warn you I've learnt a few tricks in dealing with obstreperous patients.'

'Go on!' he derided, again filling up her glass. 'I may also have learnt a few tricks to deal with nurses who have already dealt with obstreperous patients. I've knocked you out, once, remember, and that was before we were so well acquainted. Just anything could happen from now on. I feel I must warn you, Claire, not to be fooled by the intellectual aspect of my character, the diplomas, Doctorate, etcetera. I am in fact a very physical person. That fellow who married us couldn't have imagined what he was saying when he spoke about wrath. When my wrath is stirred I get fighting mad. I can't be sarcastic or moody I just want to hit hard. My mother despaired when I came home with one black eye after another.'

'You're making me nervous,' Claire teased.

'I'm also quick to demonstrate affection,' he assured her. 'There are always two sides to a coin and something of devil and angel in all of us. Well–' he looked at her briefly – 'what happens now?'

'What happens now?' she echoed, draining her glass. 'What should happen now?'

'I don't think,' he said with an odd little laugh, 'that you expect me to take you off to some hotel where I would proceed to ravish you? I mean it's not that sort of a do, is it?'

She went very white and said, 'No. It's not that sort of a "do", as you call it.'

She stood up, but the champagne had been too much for her on top of everything else and she staggered. He brought her up firmly against his chest and pressed his warm cheek to her cold one.

'I'm sorry, Claire, my dear. I didn't mean to upset you. I'm a little lost as to what to do or say. You appear very contained and cool but I'm in a ferment. After all, I haven't been married before. You must excuse me.'

'Do you think–' she asked – 'you could manage to take me somewhere for a bite of lunch? I didn't take breakfast and don't know when I last ate and the champagne just about accounted for my legs. As I feel at present you could very easily carry me off to some hotel and – and ravish me, without me knowing a thing about it. But I put you on your honour not to do so, because when – or if – you ever do, I want to be there and playing my part. Understood?'

'Hoist with me own petard, by Gad!' he said admiringly, and set her back gently, as if she was made of porcelain, on her own two feet. 'You give as good as you get, don't you? Right! Well, I think I must take you back with me to college for a snack. The restaurants will be crowded out and this pub doesn't do meals. Come on! We have to take a taxi as the jag's being overhauled ready to take us across the continent.'

'We're motoring to Switzerland?' Claire asked, deciding to go along with the pervasive dream of being a newly-married woman planning her new life.

'I think so. We'll need a goodly amount of baggage and transport at the other end.' He stopped a taxi and handed her in. 'Can you be ready in a fortnight?'

'A fortnight?' she almost squeaked.

'A fortnight, Mrs Hirst.'

'I'll try,' she said, savouring the sound of her new name for the first time. 'I have to get my passport changed, you know.'

'Well, do it in person. No delay that way. Sold the cottage, yet?'

'Not quite. Do you know that when some people came yesterday morning the woman asked to use the bathroom, and the wretched toilet wouldn't flush properly? She was standing there all pink and embarrassed and we were having a go and finally the estate agent pulled the handle and it came off in his hand. Are you laughing? It wasn't funny, I tell you. It has never happened before and–' suddenly she was laughing, too, laughing and laughing until the muscles of her empty stomach positively ached. 'I suppose it was ludicrous,' she admitted, 'especially in retrospect, as this day will be when we look back on it, how we got married and then didn't know what to do.'

'Are you,' he asked, suddenly very quietly, 'being just a little tantalizing, my dear? I think we both know what most people would do but I, personally, don't drive through red lights. It can be very dangerous.'

'No, I am not meaning to be tantalizing. When I have had something to eat I'll go back to the hotel and then home. I think we've both had quite enough excitement for one day, and the next two weeks are going to be hectic.'

Rob's rooms in college looked out upon a green quadrangle where a solitary, coal-black student sat on a mackintosh reading. A scout had been sent to bring what he could from the kitchens. He arrived back with a large tray containing a dish of various cooked meats and a bowl of salad, bread, butter and a hunk of cheese. Finally he fished two cans of beer from his jacket pockets.

'Will that suffice, Doctor?'

'Very well indeed, Bowker. You will remember I'm expecting the Master for four o'clock tea?'

'Yes, Doctor.' The scout looked frankly at Claire, who was admiring the panelling of the walls.

'My wife, Bowker.'

'Oh, yes, Doctor? I never knew you was married.'

'You see?' Rob was forking meat on to a plate and indicating that Claire should sit down and eat once the scout had left. 'I must look old and harrassed already. It never occurred to Bowker that it only happened today.'

'It is a very ageing experience,' Claire teased. 'You look every bit of twenty-nine.'

'Well, considering I'm nearly thirty-three, I shan't grieve too much. How's the wedding breakfast?'

'Great. I didn't realize how hungry I was.'

'I suppose I should have laid on a feast. Was I remiss?'

'No. This is fine. Better than eating with a lot of strangers present.'

After the meal she wandered about, entered a bedroom.

'Going somewhere?' she asked, noting the open trunks lying half packed.

'I'm leaving my rooms today. The College Master is joining me for tea and then it's farewell, Oxford.'

'Oh! I shan't know where to find you. Where *will* you be?'

'Here and there, up to London and then home to see my parents I expect. The main thing is I'll know where to find *you*.'

'Won't you be sorry to leave all this?' She felt the mattress to see how soft it was and it wasn't.

'Wasn't it you who said one should never look back? That having made up one's mind there must be no faltering?'

'I may have done.' She turned suddenly as a sixth sense warned her to face him. There was an odd gleam in his eyes and she found herself seized in a grip of steel and hurled backwards on to the hard bed. Her shoes flew off in opposite directions as she struggled briefly and then lay still as nothing else happened only the breath was squeezed out of her lungs.

She looked up at him and he was smiling with a kind of invitation.

'Rob?' she queried. 'You're heavy.'

'Well?' he asked. 'Haven't you been trained to deal with obstreperous patients? Where's your bag of tricks?'

'Oh, no!' she gasped weakly.

'Oh, yes. You were boasting, weren't you?'

She bit her lip as she glanced up at him again and then, with difficulty, filled her lungs and gathered her muscles. Her right knee, as it came up sharply, caught him below the belt and he grimaced in pained surprise. She almost succeeded in rolling off the bed but he was quicker. He pinioned her

189

arms behind her and pulled her back under him so that she couldn't again move her legs. She tried to wriggle this way and that but for the moment they were not playing, but fighting, and when she saw there was no point to it she stopped resisting.

'You see?' he, too was breathing hard from the struggle. 'With one hand behind my back I have you completely under my control.' From waving his free hand triumphantly he brought it down to her chest and undid the top button of her dress, then the second. She turned her head on one side on the rock-hard pillow and tried not to imagine they were half-way through a red light. Men and women were not meant to play fighting games because something else, dangerous and violent, was now stirring between them. Without love it had an earthy name.

'Rob?' she now appealed, and added, 'please, no. Not now.'

His own eyes were dark, she suddenly saw, and wondered how bright blue eyes could hold such shadows at times.

'No, of course,' he quickly agreed, easing away from her. 'As you said, we've had enough excitement for one day.'

He retrieved her shoes and insisted on putting them on for her, while she self-consciously fastened up the buttons of her dress.

'My goodness!' he decided, as she stood up and smoothed herself down. 'I think I just happened along in time. At any moment it might have been an obstreperous patient who took advantage of you, and then you might not have got away as you did.'

She thought about it, pulled on her little hat, picked up her bag and replied.

'I wouldn't have been married to an obstreperous patient, would I? I think I may still have pulled a trick or two out of the bag in *that* eventuality.' She waited for Bowker to announce that he had a taxi waiting for her and then smiled mischievously in the open doorway. 'Even if he *had* got one free hand behind his back,' she told him, and walked jauntily off down the long, stone corridor.

'Claire?' he called after her.

She turned, still smiling. He approached her waving a sheet of parchment.

'Marriage lines,' he said. 'You'll need those for your new passport. Don't imagine you'll always be walking out on me,' he said quietly, 'so wipe that smug little smile off your lovely pansy face.'

'Is that a threat or a promise?' she wanted to know, and was relieved – for her own sake – that Bowker came to see what the hold-up was at that moment, and fled.

She opened the cottage door and was relieved to find the unhappy ghost had gone. She had exorcised it, or she and Rob together. The evening sun shone into the yellow lounge and she had picked up a note from the doormat informing her that Mr and Mrs Morgan had fallen in love with the cottage – in spite of the toilet episode – and were proposing to put down a deposit on the morrow, if she was agreeable.

She went round the whole house singing softly, while her mind was in a kind of ferment about storing furniture and the like, and then entered the bedroom and decided to slip out of her finery and just relax.

'After all, it is my wedding day,' she pondered.

She looked at the large bed with its pink spread of Nottingham lace and wondered if Rob came to see her if they would be able to keep out of it, especially when they both knew that such a delicious fever was possible between them.

'I ought to be ashamed of such thoughts,' she told herself and then wondered why she should. 'Rob's nice and he's a gentleman and I think – in his way – he's already quite fond of me. I – I do like him. He's so – unexpected.' She felt her cheeks suffuse as she remembered how – to her own surprise – she had unexpectedly wanted to linger in that pool of heat they had created together, with his hand on her flesh under the dress and her lips denying aloud what her awakening body was demanding, silently and relentlessly.

'Only a gentleman would have let me go,' she decided, with a little toss of her head. 'After all, we *are* married and he could demand his rights. But I rather think–' she looked at herself in the mirror as she sat in her petticoat, and decided to shame the devil – 'that the way I felt today he won't exactly have to demand anything of me in future. Father always said one should never suppress one's emotions or they withered, that grief, love, sensuality all had their part to play in one's make-up. Well, I've known grief this year, and so has Rob, and today we discovered our sensuality. Maybe this will eventually lead us to the loving. I mustn't be squeamish and I don't want to be, not with a man as exciting as he is. When I agreed to marry him I thought of it as a sort of contract convenient to us both, and emotion didn't come into it. I even offered myself to him on a platter, rather as though the essential me wouldn't be in the body concerned. But I'm beginning to think, after today, Rob Hirst doesn't want half-measures in anything, and especially his marriage. If I didn't know already I was a fully paid-up member of the opposite sex then he has left me in no doubt. Some of the things I said! I didn't know I had it in me! I think I'm going to *enjoy* being married to him, and that much I hadn't allowed for.

Her hair positively gleamed as she brushed it before bed. It rose in a kind of halo, crackling with electricity, as she felt her life was doing at the moment.

EIGHT

Next day her excitement diminished somewhat, even though the sale of the house was furthered and she could now safely leave all in her solicitor's hands, as he wielded power-of-attorney for her. By late evening she was wondering why he hadn't rung her – meaning Rob. Surely after yesterday he would want to say hello, if nothing else? He knew where she was, as he had observed, but she had no idea of his whereabouts.

The second day passed likewise un-eventfully and she even felt a little hurt by his neglect. He had seemed to be quite excited by the idea of being a married man, and yet didn't he realize he had had to have a partner in this event and that she might expect him to acknowledge her existence.

The third day trailed by and she bit her lip and endured. She had 'phoned up the Passport Office and asked what documents she would need to change her existing passport, and had made an appointment to see an official on the morrow. If Rob 'phoned while she was out, then too bad. He couldn't expect her to be hanging on to the other end of the 'phone when he did condescend to get in touch.

All the way up to London she reviewed the events of that wedding day, wondering if she had imagined most of them. Actually not knowing a person very well before becoming significantly involved with him put one at a disadvantage. He could be the biggest confidence trickster of all time, and she, in her innocence, the greatest dupe ever to fall to one. She sought in her handbag and pulled out the marriage certificate. It certainly looked real enough and that *had* been a genuine register office and an authentic registrar. She read the words on the certificate: Robert Nathaniel Hirst, and under it her own name, Claire Elizabeth Matthews; their ages were thirty two and twenty-four respectively at the time of marriage. His profession was entered as College Tutor and hers as State-Registered nurse, and then came their addresses again at the time of their marriage; so Rob's was the college he had now left; his father's name and occupation were given as Sir Robert Hirst (Bart) H.M. County Court Justice, and hers simply as deceased. She hadn't even been aware that Rob's family were titled until she had read the certificate at leisure on the evening of the wedding day. The witnesses – she could picture them now, smiling and nudging each other – were Trevor and Catherine Butcher. At least *they* probably knew each other quite well by now, she thought a little cynically.

She couldn't learn much more of Rob's true intentions regarding her from the certificate, and though she had had no encouragement to get in touch with him she toyed with the idea of tracing his father in

Who's Who, ringing up the family home, and if Rob was in simply telling him she had a new passport and then leave the conversational ball in his court thereafter.

'No, I won't,' she as quickly decided. 'I won't give him the satisfaction of thinking I care one way or the other whether he keeps in touch with me or not.'

She had gone up to town on a day when Old Charlie was on hand and he had instructions to answer the 'phone and take any message.

'Well, Charlie?' she asked on her return to the cottage. 'Did anybody 'phone?'

'Yes, Mm. One wrong number and your solicitor. 'E wants you tell 'im were you bank. Will that be all, Mm?'

'Yes, Charlie. That will be all for today. You do know the new people want you to stay on, don't you? Just as long as you feel like it.'

'Thank you, Mm. But I think I just might put me feet up now that I'm nearin' seventy-five. It was just for you I came, like. You bein' so pretty an' reminding me of my daughter wot died.'

'Thanks at least for that, Charlie. I feel quite cheered up.'

But when the old man had left she cried a little.

A full week to the day after becoming Mrs Robert Nathaniel Hirst, Claire answered the doorbell with a feeling of a fire having been lit behind her eyes. She would tell him what she thought of him, if her visitor was Rob, and no mistake.

She looked up disbelievingly into the wry-smiling countenance of Dr David Gaunt, who had been best man at her marriage to Pete and with him, drinking, on the same night when Pete had driven off to his death.

'Hello, Dave!' she greeted. 'Are you coming in?'

'If I may. I wondered how you felt about seeing me. At first I thought you were going to hit me.'

'I did feel like hitting somebody,' she told

him, 'but certainly not you. How's General Practice?'

'Oh, not bad. It's so long since any of our crowd saw you that I wondered if everything was all right. I know you asked to be left alone for awhile, then I heard you were back at work, and next thing that you'd left to take a holiday. I thought I could risk calling to see that all's well after all this time, and as I have a day off...?'

'I'm over Pete's loss, Dave, if that's what you really mean. Don't worry about me. I'm going abroad for a bit, actually.' She wondered whether to tell him she had married again, but that would be rather difficult and the news would spread like wild-fire and probably be misinterpreted. 'Will you join me for tea or would you like a real drink?'

'I'll have tea, thank you. I like to be careful when I'm driving.'

She caught his eye and they both felt momentarily disconcerted as she filled the kettle and plugged it in.

'I know you blame yourself in part for Pete's death, Dave,' she said quietly, 'but we both know what he was like. He just wouldn't be told by anybody what to do or how to behave. You told him he ought to be getting back to me, as it was our wedding night and I'd be expecting him, and he chose to buy another round, and another, and so it happened. After all, if we could foresee accidents there would never be any, would there? You weren't Pete's keeper, you were his friend. Now we won't talk about it any more, but if it has made you careful when you're driving, and others, then some good might have come out of it all.'

She had prepared a salad previously, and now produced a plate of ham and chicken slices, garnished with hard-boiled eggs.

'Tuck in' she invited, pouring the tea, 'and tell me about everything and everybody.'

Dave stayed until after six and then said he must leave as he was dining with the 'firm's' receptionist.

'Smashing little red-head,' he told her as

she opened the door for him. She was smiling. When Doctor Gaunt had been at St Columba's he had always had a thing about red-haired women, natural or contrived.

'You haven't changed, Dave,' she told him.

'Nor have you, Claire, I'm happy to say, only for the better. You've come through it all like a real little trouper.' He suddenly swept her up and kissed her soundly, and somehow wetly, like a puppy, and because he was a very solid young man she couldn't do much about it. He set her down, looking very intense, and said, 'Thanks, Claire. You're a real little lady.'

A voice came from close at hand, a little amused, a little challenging and a trifle impertinent.

'Now is the time for all good men and true to say, "That's no lady, that's my wife," I do believe.'

Claire looked at Rob in disbelief for a moment, then at the jag parked some way down the lane because of Dave's car occupying the small turn-in near the front gate.

'A friend of yours?' Dave asked, with his one-sided grin.

'Robert Hirst,' she introduced in a dead sort of voice. 'David Gaunt, M.D. Well, so long, Dave, and good luck with the red-head.'

She sensed Rob following her into the hall and that fire in her head was rekindled. She turned and let fly:

'You think you can turn up when you like–' she began, and then found he had passed her and was in the kitchen, surveying the remains of the meal and helping himself to a home-made scone – 'and then make idiotic remarks in front of my friends? Just whom do you think you are?'

'Who,' he corrected her blandly. 'The nominative case is who. Who do I think I am? I *know* who I am. I'm not suffering from amnesia. These are very good. I'll have another.'

'You come here,' she proceeded, 'when at last you decide to, walk into *my* house and eat *my* food–'

'I came to take you home to dinner and meet the family, actually. Eating your food is a bonus I didn't allow for.'

He sat on the sink top and munched.

'Look here!' she challenged him. 'Just you look here!' Because he was so far above her she drummed her balled fists angrily on his knees until he fastidiously dusted crumbs from his hands, and held her off. 'Seven days–' she choked – 'for seven long days you haven't cared whether I was alive or dead, and then you turn up, out of the blue, being funny in front of a very dear old friend, and making him think goodness knows what, and then – then you walk in here, offering no explanations, and say you've come to take me to meet your family? *I'm* not your puppet. *I* don't jump when you tell me to.'

'So I take it you don't want to come? Very well–' he jumped down from the sink and strode purposefully towards the front door.

'Don't you dare walk out on me when I'm talking to you!' She was almost weeping with anger, now, backed against the front door preventing him leaving. 'I've waited a week for this, to tell you what I think of you. I – I'm very disappointed in you,' and then the tears came and she was lost.

He gathered her to his chest and said, 'I didn't mean to disappoint you, Claire. How come? What have I done?'

'What haven't you done, you mean. I thought you might have rung, or something.'

'Oh? Why? Was there some problem?'

'No. No problem.' She was losing some hypothetical argument and knew it. She had minded when he obviously didn't know he was causing offence. A continent separated them where understanding was concerned. 'I just thought you'd have called, or rung, or even written. It's a big thing being told you're going abroad in a fortnight and then not knowing, for sure, if everything's going ahead.'

'Oh, yes, it's going ahead. I've had a very busy week, but I've got the tickets for the ferry and everything. I've even booked us in

207

overnight half-way across France at an old inn. Also I've been visiting the sick. A chum of mine, from University days, with whom I was staying in town, decided to start a belly-ache in the middle of one night which, by morning, was a roaring peritonitis. It was touch and go by the time I got him into St Thomas's; but now they say he's going to be all right in time. *You* should have been there when he started with the pains. Your expertise would have been invaluable.'

She felt a little ashamed and looked down at her feet.

'Why did you let me behave like a shrew?' she asked. 'Screaming at you and hitting you the way I did.'

'Is that unusual then?' he asked in reply. 'You aren't always like that?'

She never knew when he was teasing but answered him seriously.

'I have never been like that. I've been a positive mouse. You said there was devil and angel in all of us, and I suppose that was my devil coming out. I have been working myself up all week about what I considered to be your gross neglect of me.'

'Really? I didn't think you'd expect anything of me. I told you, over lunch at the Trout, that after the wedding I would have to neglect you for a week or two. Don't you remember?'

'Yes, I do seem to remember, now.' She felt a bit of a fool and tried to retrieve the situation. 'Call it post-wedding nerves on my part. I'm sorry about your friend. That must have been very worrying for you. What did you say about dinner?'

'Well, it's entirely up to you, of course, but for once the family's all together for the evening, apart from Frances, who may turn up later. I thought we might make our announcement.'

'You mean you haven't told anybody we're married?'

'No. I thought it might be fun if we did it together.'

'Fun?' she demanded, not believing her ears.

'Yes. You don't know my family. We have been brought up very liberally. They're not the sort of folk who would expect the white satin, veil and top-hat sort of a do. We tried all that with Tom and Henrietta, when they married, and it was a complete disaster. Father, who'd been on the circuit, turned up at the wrong church in the wrong town and missed the whole thing, one bridesmaid was absent with the measles and the other threw hysterics and Ben, who was the best man, had left the ring in his other suit. At the finish Henry, my sister-in-law, tripped over her dress and went off on a very tearful honeymoon with her broken ankle in plaster. After that Ben opted for a register office do, though he did tell the family in case they wanted to be present. Father said not likely, he was playing golf that weekend, but Mother and Frances attended, I believe. So it will be mildly pleasurable to present them with a *fait accompli* and nobody will say "Oh, why didn't you tell us?" I can assure you.' He looked down at her. 'I can tell them on my own, of course,' he told her, 'and keep you tucked away so that they can merely speculate about you.'

'No,' she suddenly jutted her chin. 'I don't know that it's going to be fun but I prefer to be there in person. I'll be fifteen minutes changing. It's not formal, is it?' she turned on the stairs to ask.

'No,' he said, looking up from an appreciation of her dainty ankles to her questioning face, 'never on Tuesdays.'

'You never told me,' said Claire in dismay, surveying the rambling red-brick house set in five acres, 'you lived in such splendour.'

'Splendour?' he laughed as he handed her out of the car. 'Don't you believe it. We can't afford to have heating installed. The place is frigid in winter. Father brought us all up to take a daily cold bath so that we would never notice.'

In August, however, hung with roses and festooned with Virginia creeper, the Old Hall looked utterly charming. It had a large, red-tiled hall with an open fireplace and a suit of armour minus a breast-plate. 'Father never did find out which one of us swiped that,' Rob said. 'Ben shoved it up my pullover one day and proceeded to pelt me with his air-gun, which horrified cook and brought on one of her "turns". We examined the breast-plate, later, and it was dented all round the heart. I don't know what we did with it as we were a bit scared. Come on and meet them.'

Claire felt a hollow sensation in her middle as they entered a comfortable lived-in-looking room from which emanated a buzz of conversation.

'Hello, everybody,' Rob said clearly. 'I thought you might like to meet my wife. Come on, Claire.'

There was the shortest of pauses and then a rush of feet. A tall, plain woman in glasses said, 'I'm Henrietta. Henry, to the family. What a pair of slyboots you've been.' She kissed Claire happily. 'This is Mavis,' she introduced.

'Hello, Claire!' greeted the other sister-in-law, who was so tiny she made Henry look like a police sergeant and Claire felt quite tall as she stooped to kiss her.

'Claire? Welcome to the mad-house,' greeted Tom, who was tall and broad with a hint of paunch and almost bald. 'Jammy blighter,' he accused his smiling youngest brother. 'You've landed on your feet, as usual.'

'My dear Claire!' Ben was an older edition of Rob though not quite so tall. He kissed her robustly though Tom had merely put his lips to her hand. Rob eventually hauled him off.

'That'll do,' he said. 'The poor girl hasn't had her dinner yet.' He looked towards a chair in the corner where the *Guardian* quivered for a moment.

'That's Dad, but he's as deaf as a post,' he whispered.

'I heard that!' came from behind the *Guardian*. 'As if there weren't enough twittering women in this family!'

213

Rob looked at Claire, who smiled quickly as though telling him she understood.

'Come and meet Ma,' he invited.

'Ma' was still beautiful and in that Scandinavian way which two of her sons had inherited. She had the same bright blue eyes and an impish grin. Her hair was snow-white and bountiful and she was wiping her hands on an apron as Claire was introduced.

'Well! How nice!' she decided, taking her new daughter-in-law's hands and looking her up and down.

'Ma! She's not going to Crufts,' Rob objected. 'Ma's a judge of terriers in shows,' he confided. 'She used to breed them before we got too much for her.'

'She's very pretty,' Lady Hirst decided. 'What do you want first, dear, a girl or a boy?'

Claire flushed and her mouth dropped open.

'We thought twins,' Rob answered for her, 'one of each. It can all be arranged, now, you know, Ma, on the National Health.'

'Yes, well. I think we're ready for dinner,' said Lady Hirst. 'You can come and help load the trolley, Rob. Cook's had to go and put her legs up.'

Claire was beginning to think it hadn't been at all bad when a faint cough came from behind her.

'Well, m'dear?' said Sir Robert in an extremely judicial voice. 'So you've made an honest man of that young whipper-snapper, eh? Hm! Is he making you happy?' Claire's chin wobbled, but she didn't speak. 'If I thought he wasn't I'd thrash him, d'you hear? Within an inch of his life.'

'Gangway!' called Rob, emerging from the kitchen pushing a laden trolley. 'Oh! So you two have met.'

'May I?' Sir Robert offered his arm and Claire took it, dimpling, as the others arrived en route for the dining-room.

'We won't wait for Fanny,' said Lady Hirst. 'She may come, or not. You know what these modern girls are like. Robert, are you going to monopolize Claire or sit in your proper place?'

'Don't ask damn' silly questions, Maggie.' Sir Robert saw Claire seated and then sat down beside her so that Rob, after a moment's hesitation, sat at the head of the table.

Claire found herself thawing towards her father-in-law as he very cleverly pumped her about herself, much as though she had been a witness in one of his courts. He seemed pleased that her father had been a churchman and listened as she talked about her life at home and then her job.

Time seemed to fly and they were some-how all back in the drawing-room again, drinking coffee. Sir Robert had returned to his paper, though now it lay over his face and it looked as though he could be napping. Rob had asked who wanted brandy or liqueur, and was at a side-table pouring out. Mavis was telling Claire of the difficult time she had had producing her elder daughter, who was now nine, when there was an interruption. A girl in a floral kaftan swept into the room and called out 'Hi!' She was dark-haired and classically beautiful, but with the unmistakable blue Hirst eyes.

'Fanny!' Lady Margaret arose to embrace her daughter and the others called out greetings, apart from the figure under the *Guardian,* who had managed to signal he would like a brandy but now made no move.

'And look what I found looking all lost and lorn in London's fair city–' Frances proceeded, and signalled to someone to enter the room – 'yours, I believe, Rob? I don't care a damn what differences there have been between you, lately, but I think it's time you stopped playing silly twits and made up.'

The tall fair-haired girl with the chocolate-drop eyes, who had entered the room on Frances' heels, had no eyes for anybody but Rob, who was standing as though petrified with a brandy glass in one hand and a liqueur in the other. She reached to kiss him firmly on the lips and then said, so that everybody could hear 'I know I was in the wrong, Rob, and I freely admit it. But you must forgive me. You must.'

Lady Hirst was the first one to react and she did so with admirable composure and dignity. Drawing Claire to her feet she led her forward.

'Fanny, dear, you haven't met your new sister-in-law, have you? She's Rob's wife and her name's Claire.'

As though in slow motion Claire saw Angela Dane's brown eyes widen in horror and shock and anger and Rob looking as though he wore a mask, devoid of all expression and life.

'But she can't be!' Angela denied ringingly, and turned back to Rob. 'It's too soon. You've done this to punish me, haven't you? You don't love *her*. You *can't*.' Then she turned and ran headlong from the room.

It seemed to Claire that she was only at times present during the next hour's shenanegans at the Old Hall. Judge Hirst had emerged from under his paper and was sitting beside her on the sofa, holding her hand and occasionally patting it. He had advised those who wished to disturb his peace to do it elsewhere, and there were sounds of furious exchanges and sobs from other parts of the house and the clatter of dishes from the kitchen where 'Henry' and Mavis were doing the washing-up.

'I shouldn't worry, you know,' said Sir Robert, with another pat. 'I don't know what there is about that boy but girls always did swarm after him. I'm glad he's married you. It's time he settled down.'

'I really think I ought to be going home, soon,' said Claire after a while.

'I'll go and get Rob, my dear. You're very welcome to stay the night, you know.'

It was Frances who came into the drawing-room first, however, her blue eyes blazing.

'Well! I don't know what you're playing at, I'm sure, but it's something rather rum. He was going to marry Angela about six weeks ago and now he's married to you. Don't say your eyes met across a crowded room and that was that. I can imagine my fool brother being upset by some row they had and ready to rebound, but what's your excuse? Were you on the rebound, too?'

Claire merely looked unhappy as Rob appeared and marched across the room, grabbing her roughly.

'Come on, Claire! We're getting out of here. I forgot to tell you that my sister is really quite civilized when she tries to be.' In the hall Claire was kissed by the brothers and sisters-in-law and then Lord and Lady Hirst with a most tender affection as they all said goodnight.

'Could you put me up for the night?' Rob asked in the car. 'I mean have you a guest-room or even a sofa? If I go back home I'll probably strangle young Fanny.'

'You can have the guest-room,' she said. 'Rob, did you marry me on the rebound?'

'I suppose I did. What else would you call it?'

'That's what Frances said. She asked me

what my excuse was.'

'It's not as she implies.'

'Angela appeared to still be desperately in love with you. The way she flung herself on you to kiss you. It seemed to go on and on.'

'I could hardly do anything about it with a glass in either hand. It seemed to go on and on for me, too.'

'It's not very nice seeing another woman kissing your husband, I discovered. Though I have no real right to mind.'

'It's not very nice seeing another fellow kissing your wife, as I discovered earlier this evening. Right or not I *did* mind.'

The car shushed to a standstill in front of Walnut Cottage.

'I think we'd better go back to square one,' Claire said later that evening as they drank cocoa together. 'Do we carry on, as though nothing had happened, or think again?'

'We carry on in spite of *everything* that's happened,' Rob said quietly. 'It's obvious I haven't made a mountaineer of you, yet, Claire. One is taught never to look back.'

NINE

The big car ate up the miles of northern France, and Claire was quite enchanted by it all. She had never travelled on the continent by car, before, and it was quite different. She exclaimed as the famous landmarks of the two world wars cropped up as real places. Vimy Ridge, Cambrai and the cemeteries of Normandy with the tiny white crosses marching in neat rows sometimes into infinity. The villages, too, were so different to English communities. Gardens were the exception rather than the rule; it seemed the order of things to keep chickens and a few fat geese rather than grow dahlias and roses. They went through Arras, the first sizeable town on their route, or, rather, they went round and round Arras, waved on by agitated traffic policemen in a one-way system from which there appeared to be no escape, and they laughed as they finally turned off and – with luck – saw a signpost putting them on the road to St Quentin.

'Sleep if you want to,' Rob advised, 'we had a very early start and there's a long way to go.'

She didn't really feel sleepy but closed her eyes only to wonder afresh at the turn her life had taken since she had met this man who was now her husband, albeit in name only. She was under no illusions that he loved her; the thought had crossed her mind after the events of the wedding day that he desired her; but all that excitement was a sort of fool's gold, she had now concluded, and not to be confused with the real thing. When Rob had spent that night in the cottage she hadn't quite known what to expect; he had that effect on one; but though she had not turned the lock on her door – because she had in a wild moment promised never to do so – he had apparently slept soundly in the guest-room untroubled by her proximity and the fact that she was legally his wife. He had come back for another night, 'phoning first to ask if she had any 'kissing cousins' from the hospital visiting her, so that she could give them due notice to clear out, but when he arrived he looked tired, and had gone early to bed, and again had not sought her out. The following morning she was winding up her affairs for the year ahead and he had insisted on accompanying her to the solicitor's and to the bank. She had introduced him to officials as her husband and been congratulated.

'I'm so very happy for you, Mrs Hirst,' her solicitor had said, 'and you, sir, are a very lucky man.'

At the bank she had drawn traveller's cheques and been surprised to find she had so much in her account, as the house-purchase had still not been legally completed.

'A deposit of a thousand pounds from Mr

R.N. Hirst,' the bank manager told her.

'Oh! My husband,' she said in some confusion. 'Of course.'

Outside the bank she had said, 'Rob, you don't have to *pay* me to carry out this contract. It was to our mutual, even though temporary, advantage, we both agreed.'

'In my family,' Rob said sternly, 'a husband supports his wife, even though she should be a Rothschild heiress. While you're my wife I shall look after you befittingly. If you decide to get a job, then that's your own to do with what you like. Now don't let's argue about money.'

'But you said you hadn't much – as a family, I mean.'

'That's true. But I have recently inherited my maternal grandmother's estate, due to being forced to suck up to her as a child, and now I'm laughing.'

'So I've married a millionaire!' she joked. 'Good for me!'

'Not exactly,' he said. 'Twenty-five thousand, less what used to be called death duties, and a dark little house in Putney where I must continue to maintain Grandma's genteel old companion in a style befitting. I'll probably be out of pocket in the end.'

'You're an old sentimentalist!' she accused.

'You're going to learn, over the next year, that I'm not just a pretty face, my dear,' he had responded meaningfully.

She rolled her head to regard St Quentin through her lashes as they took the *toutes directiones* route round the outskirts. She was on the brink of sleep when Rob said, 'Claire! Laon ahead. It's one of the sights you mustn't miss.'

She looked in amazement and wonder at the historical city set on its hill, within ancient walls, with a cathedral which looked as though it was made out of Brussels lace.

Shortly afterwards he pulled the car into a wooded turn-off and suggested they have a cup of coffee. She had packed a flask and some ham and tomato sandwiches; they had

had breakfast on the ferry, having left the cottage at six a.m. for Dover, and as this had meant Claire rising at four o'clock, Rob must have been up even earlier if he had been to bed at all.

He now said, as he drunk the steaming coffee and accepted a second sandwich, 'I shall be glad to put my head on a pillow tonight, and no mistake.'

'Would you let me drive for a bit, Rob?' He stared at her in surprise. 'Father had an Aston-Martin – a big, heavy old thing – which I learnt to drive in, and I often drove Pete's Mercedes. That was power-assisted, like the Jag, but I'll understand if you can't bear the idea, of course.'

'Why not?' he said, with a slow smile of appreciation. 'Just remember she accelerates like Concorde when overtaking, so use her power with discretion, that's a good girl.'

She was a little nervous, naturally, as she drove the big, highly powered car and felt the power under her foot, so that it was difficult to keep from breaking the speed limit on straight lengths of poplar-lined roads. The juggernauts were a bug-bear on these roads, and it was very nervously that she overtook the first of many, but the acceleration was, as Rob had said, so immediate, that she was soon taking such obstacles in her stride. When her navigator dropped off to sleep she smiled to think he had such confidence in her and drove very carefully, only overtaking when she was invited to do so by the driver of the vehicle in front. Rob had said he wanted to drive through Rheims, which was difficult, and she now saw that it was a mere twenty kilometres distant and that the villages were beginning to join up, aided by new housing developments into one vast suburb. The traffic was now crawling at a steady thirty miles per hour as it congested, and there was no point in overtaking, so she stopped and started with the rest of them, hoping to find a lay-by where she could turn in and wake Rob, who had now slept for a good hour and a half and must be feeling mildly refreshed.

As her thoughts had been wandering she missed the next surge forward of the traffic and was passed by three honking motorists, looking at her indignantly, before she could find gear. They were driving through one of those dusty little French villages, without any individuality, whose front doors open on to the road and where the old sit, in open doorways, smoking or passing their time watching the traffic, and, sometimes, a grandchild. As Claire got the car moving again a tiny child suddenly ran out to retrieve a ball. An old grandmother shouted and Claire only had time to breathe a prayer before braking hard. Rob shot forward the length of his seat belt like a rag-doll, all relaxed from sleep, and Claire's ribs hurt sharply where the belt bit but the car stopped within half a yard.

'What the hell–?' Rob shouted. 'That was a stupid thing to do!'

Claire released herself, trembling, and

shot out of the car. The grandmother was holding the small child and crying but there was no sign of injury to the child, who was even now pointing at the painted ball, which still lay in the gutter. A younger woman appeared, obviously upset, and snatched the child from the grandmother's arms. She then spoke shrilly to Claire and at great length and all the time the traffic flowed past, with horns honking. Rob had appeared and took up with the Frenchwoman, patting the old one on the arm. He eventually indicated that Claire get back into the car, on the passenger side, and prepared to drive himself.

'I'm sorry,' he said at length, 'the child's mother said you stopped the car like magic and that no harm's done. She went on about the traffic and children having nowhere to play and how it's getting worse all the time, and that if Madame's reactions hadn't been so quick it could have been a tragedy. She wants you to know how thankful they all are.'

231

Claire didn't speak. She couldn't trust herself.

'Look! I've said I'm sorry,' Rob repeated. 'I hope you're not one who sulks. I didn't know what had happened. It was one hell of an awakening.'

A shudder went through Claire and – warm as the day was – goose pimples rose on her arms.

'The glove compartment,' Rob instructed, 'a silver flask. Brandy. Take a swig.'

'B – but–'

'You're a nurse and even I know the signs of shock. Take a swig or I'll have to ram it down your throat and I can't get off the road at present.'

She obediently found the flask and gulped from it. The brandy was strong and comforting. She took another swig and began to warm up once more. Her trembling ceased though Rob contrived with one hand to pull his jacket from the back seat round her shoulders.

'OK now?' he asked.

'Mm. And I don't think I sulk.'

'Good girl.'

All this was marred for her by the child's wild, weeping face continuing to appear before her. With its blonde hair and brown eyes it had looked like Angela when she had turned on Rob that night. Angela was really very lovely, and they *had* known love, she and Rob. Was he still hankering after her, only his pride keeping him from seeking her out and taking her back? Maybe his injured pride would heal in time.

They were now entering Rheims, handsome by any standards and so spacious. Claire saw famous Champagne names flaunting from buildings that looked like mediaeval turreted castles, but the cathedral proved elusive, with all its associations with Jeanne d'Arc.

'Perhaps we can take a holiday and see such things at leisure,' Rob said when she mentioned this. 'When you're travelling a thousand miles from A to B, you can't stop and look at all the wonders without taking a week over it.'

'No, I do understand,' said Claire, who had found her two and a half hour stint of driving on foreign roads rather wearing. 'How much longer before we stop for the day?'

'The *Auberge de la Voute* is about nineteen kilometres beyond Rheims. I've only heard of it from a friend. He says there's a board by the roadside, so watch out on your side.'

'That's it!' Claire announced at length. 'I'm sorry, but we've just passed it. It's on the opposite side of the road.'

It was a handsome double carriage-way at this point.

'I'll have to go on to the next loop. There!' he waited for a stream of cars to pass on their way to Rheims and then nipped into the opposite carriage-way. 'That's it!' he agreed, and turned down a narrow track through a birch wood. The old inn stood as it had obviously for centuries. There was a notice which stated there was stabling for thirty horses.

'It's lovely!' Claire exclaimed. 'What a pity we have no horses!'

A boxer dog ran out, barking, but nothing else stirred for some time and then an elderly lady beckoned them inside a dim hall, for shutters were drawn to keep out the sun, as continentals like to do.

'Up we go,' said Rob, as the old woman led the way upstairs. 'I've told her you'd appreciate a cup of tea in your room.'

'How thoughtful!' said Claire.

There were rather lengthy altercations on the dim landing though Claire saw an open bedroom door and a bed covered in roseate cretonne.

'There's been a bit of a mess up,' Rob told her awkwardly. 'I ordered two singles, but apparently all the rooms are doubles. Madame kindly pointed out that there are two beds in all rooms and that we *are* married, *n'est ce pas?* I told her I talked in my sleep and she laughed and asked what secrets I had to keep from my wife. Now I don't know what to say.'

'Oh, come on!' said Claire, entering the room, where there were indeed two quite capacious beds, and a washbasin curtained off in one corner. 'Don't make a fuss about it. This is lovely and it will do.'

'You don't think I should order another double room?'

'I certainly do not. What would Madame think?'

'It's what *you* think that worries me. You may be thinking I've planned all this.'

'Rubbish!'

A young boy came up with a tray of tea for one and a beer for Rob, who was busily unfastening the shutters and throwing them wide so that the early evening sun poured in. Swallows wheeled and dipped and as Claire joined Rob at the window the boxer dog chased off into the trees and a squirrel chattered angrily.

'Isn't this something?' Rob asked.

'Lovely. It's so peaceful. Is there time for a walk before dinner?'

'Yes. We dine at seven thirty but it'll be

good to stretch our legs. I'll leave you the facilities in the corner, there, and I'll go along to the bathroom. See you in about half an hour.'

It seemed to her odd that they should not undress in the same room where fate had decreed they should practically be sleeping together, but she washed the dust of the day away while sipping her second cup of tea, changed her clothes and was doing her hair when Rob returned, needing a clean shirt.

They walked out of the Auberge and the dog joined them, obviously glad to be going 'walkies'. They followed him down a steep slope and came to a canal, arrow-straight and disappearing under about a mile of tunnel.

'Ah!' said Rob. 'Now I see. The horses stabled at the Inn must once have pulled the barges. I suppose, now, they're all diesel-powered.'

Claire was exclaiming over wild flowers she had never seen before growing rank on the high banks. 'That should be stitchwort, but it's so big. That blue stuff must be gentian. Did you ever see such a blue?'

'Look at your eyes, my lovely,' he invited.

She flushed prettily. 'Look at your own,' she replied.

They walked for about half a mile along the tow-path and then turned to be rewarded by the sight of a barge emerging from the tunnel, with children playing on the hatches and a lurcher dog exchanging insults with Raoul, the boxer.

Back at the inn they decided to have Madame's 'special', as her chef was away on holiday. They appeared to be the only guests in residence though two parties arrived for dinner.

The 'special' was truly special in that it was most unusual. First they had chopped-up raw mushrooms in a vinaigrette sauce, then what they both thought were veal sausages, but which turned out to be 'chitterlings', and very savoury they were with thin French beans and *pommes-frites*. Finally they had raisin tart with cream.

'I'm dead,' Rob said as they refused coffee. 'I just want–'

'Me, too,' said Claire, and led the way upstairs.

This time there was no false modesty. They undressed and slid between the sheets and Rob neither talked in his sleep nor snored. Claire knew because she watched him for a long time, wondering why she had not as readily fallen into the arms of Morpheus as he.

The next day's motoring was more picturesque as they snaked through the valley of the Marne, occasionally seeing the river with its fringe of woods and lush pastures to Joinville, where they filled up with petrol, and then on to Chaumont, where history started again, to Langres, walled as Laon had been, and then frantic shopping in a small village so that they could enjoy a picnic lunch at leisure. Claire was put into the local *supermarché* to shop for butter and cheese and a light red wine while Rob went to buy a *bagette,* that bread of such excellence that it makes an English loaf seem like a steamed pudding compared. They found a small woodland stop shortly after and Rob carved up the bread, Claire spread butter and a slice of delicious local cheese and they ate biting at tomatoes in their hands.

'C'est la vie!' Rob decided as they collected up their rubbish to bury, and she wondered if he really thought it was, in her company, or if he secretly wished she had been somebody else.

Vesoul was another historical place and then they were heading for the Belfort gap which was the gateway leading to Switzerland. They were at the Customs Post in Basel by three p.m. and at five they were cruising through Luzern, which spelling Claire had now become used to as Northern Switzerland has accepted the German language without surrendering its own brand of nationalism. Now Rob was asking questions of policemen in German – he really was quite a linguist – and so they came to number three Bergestrasse, the corner of a row of old four-storey houses looking over a green, railed-in garden square. A woman greeted them at the door on to the street and told Rob where he should park the car once it was unpacked. Claire gathered by the number of brass plates that the building contained offices, mostly, and these were by now empty.

'*Ich habe auf Sie gewartet,*' she now said, producing a bunch of keys and pressing a button for the lift to descend.

'*Dankeschön,*' Rob said. 'She was told to wait for us,' Rob explained to Claire as they got into the lift, 'but now she has to rush home to cook supper for her family. And this is it,' he proceeded as the lift stopped and they got out in the hallway of what was obviously their flat. 'How's that for service, eh? This is home.'

The woman, who was Frau Schulz, tugged Claire after her to the kitchen, waved towards a bedroom and then said she must go. She gave Rob two keys, one to the flat, if they preferred to use the stairs, and one to the outer door, then she got into the lift and was gone.

Like two children they explored at leisure. There were two bedrooms, Claire noted in some relief. The bathroom was huge and there was a shower attachment; the living-room was L-shaped with one end obviously used for dining. A little iron balcony led off and Claire stood looking out over old Luzern with a handsome peak standing guard in the distance.

'That's Pilatus,' said Rob, 'I'm almost sure. I must unpack the car and shift it over there.'

'I'll help,' said Claire.

Up and down in the lift they went until all their things were inside. Claire noted that Rob took his own luggage into the smaller bedroom automatically, and decided that it was probably better to get to know one another gradually rather than to be forced by propinquity into situations they weren't ready for. She then surveyed her kitchen again, opened the door of the fridge to find it already stocked. There was milk in cartons, Emmentaale cheese, butter and black-cherry jam and sausages in the ice-box. She then looked into cupboards and found instant coffee and tea-bags, various herbs and spices.

'Well?' Rob asked over her shoulder. 'What do you think?'

'Oh, it's gorgeous. A lovely flat. I feel I want to do something. Would you like a cup of tea?'

'Why not? That would be nice. Then we'll clean up, dress up and go out to eat.'

Claire sang as she made the tea and found a packet of biscuits along with cereals in another cupboard. She didn't remember when last she had wanted to sing as she worked.

TEN

There was a week left of the long summer holiday before Rob had to start work, and Claire found herself enjoying every day of it. One day they just explored the town and marketed, and somewhat diffidently Rob shoved a small package at her.

'For you,' he said. 'Open it.'

'Here? In the street?'

'Why not? If you don't like it I can change it.'

She gazed for some time at the single, well-cut diamond glinting in its red-gold setting.

'It looks like an engagement ring,' she said.

'That's what it is. I admit not many people get engaged after they're married, but our circumstances were rather pressing. I think it might be nice to get engaged, if you've no objection?'

'I've no objection.' She tried the ring on and a tear stole down her cheek.

'It's too tight? You don't like it?' Rob asked anxiously.

'On the contrary I love it and it fits perfectly. You know you said you hadn't been married before, and became quite excited? Well, I have never been engaged before. I may not show it but it makes me feel quite excited, too. Thank you and – may I kiss you?'

Instead it was he who bent to kiss her, firstly on the lips and then, gently, on each damp cheek.

Another day they went on the lake, known locally as the Vierwaldstätter See, on a chugging steamer. Rob had told her to wear the boots he had bought for her on the previous day; 'so that I can really walk you to death'; and in spite of their weight she found them firm and comfortable and pleasurably noisy on pavements. They left the steamer and, surely enough, above the pleasant, lakeside village reared the inevitable peak.

'That's the Rigi,' Rob said, 'and I'm going to make it easy for you this time. We'll take the railway up to the hotel, have lunch, and then I'm going to start getting you in real trim.'

The little train climbed almost vertically at times, occasionally waiting on a loop-line for its partner to pass it coming down, with a mutual sounding of whistles saying hello and goodbye. Rob was explaining the principle of the railway's safety record, how there were 'teeth' which gripped the coaches and prevented them from slipping.

The view from the hotel was magnificent and a great many people had foregathered there, some from the train, others who had climbed and still more who looked as though they were guests at the scattered farms hereabouts.

'When I first came here it was June,' Rob said, 'and we were just on the snowline. It was hot in the sun but very cold in the shade. That tree was still only in bud.'

They had a fairly light meal by Swiss standards – the Swiss were great trencher-men, Claire was deciding – with *Wiener Schnitzels;* thin veal steaks dipped in breadcrumbs and fried in butter, a green salad and no sweet. They then began to climb, and it was hard going as there were no bogs on the Rigi. Looking up Claire saw the snow-cap seeming far, far off, and decided she'd never make it that far.

'Of course not,' Rob told her. 'I'm getting you into shape, not finishing you off. We'll be turning off, soon. You'll see plenty of snow in Winter at Grindelwald.'

Suddenly she stopped and sank to her knees.

'Oh, Rob, look! Crocuses at this time of year! They must be Autumn crocuses. I've heard of them, but–'

She put a yellow bloom to his neck. 'You like butter,' she laughed at him.

'So do I. And I like girls knee-deep in

yellow crocuses, too. So watch out!'

'I may not choose to,' her eyes fell under his persistent challenging stare, but when he offered her a hand to pull her to her feet she accepted it and walked on, eventually arriving at a cable-car station, from where they made a swift descent to the village and the pier-head for the sail home.

They spent another day in Bern, seeing the famous mediaeval houses with their fine external paintings, walking the covered arcades where there were shops with goods so expensive it was useless simply to ask the price of an item hopefully. They saw the bears, symbolic of the city, in their pit, and young 'teddies' in a crèche nearby.

On another day they had a visitor, the Herr Direktor Professor Gutermann, head of the International College and Rob's new boss.

'So good to see you here,' he explained, handing Claire a posy of cream roses tied with pink ribbon. 'You like our city, yes? You are a good time having?'

'Very good, thank you,' Claire said, putting the roses in a small glass jug.

'You are right,' Professor Gutermann said to Rob, nudging him in a man to man way. 'She is very pretty lady, your wife. Just as you said, I sink a "smasher" it was.'

Claire flushed, realizing that it must have been Angela Rob was speaking of at the time, but he leapt in quickly.

'Actually my wife is a very useful member of society, too, Professor. She's a trained nurse.'

'Really? Then she would like a job after the *Flitterwoche*,' he frowned in concentration as he tried to remember the English word.

'The honeymoon,' Rob prompted. 'I don't know, but I will leave all that to her. Darling?' he turned to her with a smile which asked her to excuse the extravagant endearment. 'Would you like a job? The Professor may know the hospitals around here.'

'Of course I want to work,' Claire said promptly. 'Perhaps I would take a part-time job and then I could look after the flat and do the shopping as usual?'

'The reason I asked,' said the Professor, 'is that we are needing a nurse – a matron, I sink you say – for the college. A doctor calls two mornings a week and we hold a surgery. The matron then gives injections and does dressings and hands out the headache pills. But our nurse has gone off to work in United States. We don't pay much, you see.'

'I think I would like that,' said Claire. 'But what about language problems?'

'We all speak English; every student must be competent in English and German and French before he is admitted. Well, I have very much myself enjoyed and I have also a new nurse for the college. My secretary will give you all the information in a letter, my dear Frau Hirst, and you, Doctor, goodbye for now.'

Rob went down in the lift with Herr Gutermann and Claire was smiling trium-phantly when he returned.

'Do you really want to do it?' he asked.

'Yes. I would like to be part of the college, too. It doesn't sound like a too-demanding job and I don't really want to work full time just yet. I'm enjoying being a *Hausfrau*.'

She had told him she wanted to learn German and he had promised to find her a teacher.

Usually on retiring he knocked on her door and called goodnight, but on this night he knocked and turned the handle. Her heart was pounding as she met his eyes.

'Just checking,' he said, cheerily, 'that I'm not locked out.'

He closed the door which she flew to open again.

'Rob?' she called.

'Yes, my dear?'

'I – I said I never would. There's no need for you to check. You're free to enter my room whenever you like.'

Her voice wobbled a bit at the end uncertainly.

'Thank you, Claire,' he said sincerely. 'I shall remember that,' and he went on into his own room leaving her feeling just a bit of an impulsive fool.

But on the whole the relationship was pleasant. It was sometimes like being on the coach-tour again, apart from the fact that she now knew there would be no goodbyes after a fortnight. She was sure he liked her and admitted in her own secret heart that she rather more than liked him. Seeing him first thing in the morning without his shirt on his way to the bathroom could make her feel quite dizzy, and if he slipped off to the post-office, or to buy an English newspaper, her heart leapt to see him return, though she gave no sign of this.

On the night before term started she went to bed before him, as usual. She was brushing her hair when he knocked on her door and entered the bedroom. She kept on brushing, trying not to let her feelings show.

'I like to see you doing that,' he said from behind her. 'It's very domestic and calming.'

She felt anything but domestic and calm

as, in the mirror, she saw him trying out the bed.

'It's more comfortable than mine,' he decided.

She had to forcibly stop herself from asking, 'Then why don't you stay?' in case he should reject her.

He did, however, hold her closely in his arms and then seek her lips in a long, investigatory, satisfying kiss.

'Goodnight, Claire,' he said almost abruptly, and was gone.

She stood for a moment not knowing whether to laugh or cry.

'A one-sided love affair would be too much!' she said aloud, ruefully. 'Maybe I should start locking my door and then I wouldn't appear so obvious. But the kiss was – was–' she couldn't put into words what the kiss was, but it had seemed to convey that they might not be just good friends for much longer.

Every Tuesday and Friday, under the terms

of her new appointment, Claire attended Dr Oeschker at his clinics held in the college. Students would attend with limps, after injuries in the *Turnverein*, or Gymnastic Club, or with sore throats, boils, fevers and the hundred and one things which affect the young, and a couple even attended who were declared to be one hundred per cent fit, and who had simply wanted to see the new Matron. Also members of the staff came occasionally. The Applied Mathematics master was a diabetic, and the junior French mistress had trouble with anaemia. After the clinic Claire would go to the treatment-room, where she gave injections, bandaged or splinted and gave medicines on prescription. Every day she was present for treatments for an hour in the morning, and again in the evening from six until seven p.m., even when there was no clinic. She had bought a simple blue dress for these ministrations and had packed a couple of sister's caps to bring with her. She soon fell into the routine of her days and enjoyed them. She had plenty of time for marketing; she lunched alone as Rob stayed at college with the rest for this meal; three times a week she took German lessons with a retired teacher who lived not far from Bergestrasse. She usually prepared the evening meal while she was taking a cup of tea, having cleaned round the flat meanwhile, went to do her evening session at the college and came home with Rob for dinner.

'We must think about getting you a little car of your own,' Rob said after a week of this, setting down a heavy case containing essays on Shakespeare's sonnets.

'Oh, the street-cars aren't bad, and think how fit I must be getting with all the exercise!'

'Come and sit beside me,' he invited, from where he lounged on the velvet sofa. 'Drop everything and be a good, little wife.'

'I'm not sure,' she said, with tremulous lips, 'that I want to be a good little wife. I'd rather be a happy one.'

He drew her down beside him and regarded her in amusement.

'And what makes a wife happy, may I ask?'

'Her husband's happiness. Every wife wants her husband to be happy.'

'What a sweet thought!' he decided. 'You know something–?' he didn't continue but looked at her with his eyes grown peculiarly dark.

She thought he was going to kiss her in that special, nerve-tingling way when he looked beyond her and asked, 'Is that the mail?'

'Yes,' she said, swallowing her disappointment, and handed him four letters, two with English stamps.

'Anything for you?'

'No, but I can share yours.'

He read in silence and then handed her a sheet of flimsy paper.

'Share that for a start,' he invited.

'My dearest Boo,' Claire read:

'I suppose you'll tear this up in a rage

when you know who it's from, but I'll risk it and carry on...

'...I really did get off on the wrong foot with your new wife, didn't I? The family gave me all sorts of hell after you'd left that night. Pa told me to get that strumpet out of the house – meaning Angela, whom he hadn't taken to at all – and to write a letter of apology to Claire, immediately, to whom he had taken in a big way. In fact I had to hear Claire's praises sung from everybody and I must admit that I didn't know about the Kevin episode when I acted as I did. Angela told me that he swept her off her feet like a lightning storm and it was as quickly over. I didn't know that she stood you up, either. But I'm still not sure where Claire fits in as it was all a bit quick, wasn't it, Boosy, darling? But your affair, entirely, and I shall say no more. If you're still interested in your little Fanny, I start my articles with Wiggs, Marchant & Kemp the first week in October. I would like to come out and see you, maybe stay in the love-nest for a week if you can stand the idea. I can manage an air-ticket but not a hotel, so tell me what you think.

'My apologies to Claire. I do feel a fool about all that. I really do...

Love,

Frances.'

'Well?' Rob asked.

'I suppose she'll have to come,' Claire said, somehow managing to flounce off the sofa. 'She's your sister and of course she must feel free to visit her own brother. Boo, I think she said?'

'Her name for me, it needn't be yours.'

'Where's she going to sleep?'

'Aha! Now, where?'

'Well, obviously in your room, and you must move in with me. I still can't get over the feeling that your sister is looking for flaws in our marriage of haste, and to think we weren't sleeping together would give her something to speculate about.'

'And *will* we be sleeping together, in the

true sense, I wonder?'

Claire turned and her cheeks were blazing.

'I shouldn't think so with her – a spy – in the flat. After all, we've managed not to for nearly two months, even when we were in twin beds in the same room. I should think squeezed into a single bed we'd still manage not to. Don't you? As you once said, it's not that sort of a do, is it?'

He looked at her wearing what she privately called his D. Litt expression, faintly distastefully.

'You know, Claire, when you're angry you can be quite nasty.'

'I know. It must be my devil again.' She looked down at her hands which she was clenching and unclenching agitatedly. 'It's just that there are some things I can't bear treating lightly, Rob. You are inclined to make private jokes of very serious situations.'

'Then I'm sorry. I will try not to offend you again. Perhaps you have never heard of the clown who laughs to hide his pain. I will write to Fanny telling her to get lost.'

He, too, was up off the sofa like a jack-in-the-box.

'No! No!' Claire almost wept. 'You are not to do that. She would conclude it was me behind everything. She's your sister and she loves you. That's why she attacked me the way she did. I think her reference to the love-nest was a bit derisory but I don't care to have other people thinking there's something wrong with our marriage.'

'But there is, isn't there, Claire?'

'What do *you* think?' she flared, tears running down her cheeks. 'What would anybody think if they knew the way we live?'

'I really thought we were living rather nicely. This morning I actually felt happy.' He began to pace about like a caged tiger.

'Don't *do* that,' she almost screamed, 'or I shall hit you!'

He suddenly faced her and they stared each other out for a full minute.

'We're having a quarrel, Claire,' he decided, his voice level. 'In all marriages there has to be a first row. I believe people say all the things they don't really mean–?' He looked at her invitingly. 'You didn't really mean–?'

'Dinner's been ready for over half an hour,' she told him, mopping her eyes. 'Whatever we mean or don't mean we can't waste good meat at the prices we pay here.' He followed her to the kitchen where she strained the too-soggy cabbage and mashed the potatoes because they had fallen, and then she felt a little ashamed and relented.

'Fancy having our first row about your sister coming to stay! I *am* sorry. She's very welcome. I shall enjoy getting to know her better.'

But though they very quickly made up, something had been hurt in the relationship. Rob started to bring her posies home, or delicious *pralinés* and even a thin, half-wild kitten he had almost run over, which they named Thomas, and had to rename Thomasina very quickly. But the goodnight kisses stopped, and her bedroom door handle didn't turn. He called goodnight, as before, in passing. Then, the day before Frances was to come, he automatically carried his things into the larger bedroom and asked Claire which side of the bed she preferred.

He didn't come to bed until after midnight and she feigned sleep. She felt the bed dip under his weight and then he was very quickly asleep whereas she was suddenly staringly wide awake.

'I have never slept with a man, before,' she thought, miserably, 'and I certainly never dreamt it would be like this when I did.'

Frances's visit was of the curate's egg variety as far as Claire was concerned. She and Rob arrived laughing merrily, from the airport at Zurich, but Claire felt very much the outsider as he showed his sister round the flat and then the view from the balcony, rather as though it was of the promised land.

'And this is Claire, my wife,' he finally said

jokingly, and Frances looked the other full in the face.

'Yes, of course, it's Claire. I'm sorry about that other time, as I think Rob will have told you. Forgive me?'

'Of course,' Claire smiled. 'You were not to know and it must have been a shock.'

'Well, not actually a shock. Our family has always been mad and done strange things. I was surprised because Angela threw herself upon me asking me to intervene.' She looked from Rob to Claire uncertainly. 'I take it the subject of Angela is taboo?' she asked.

'Not necessarily. I don't mind,' said Claire sweetly.

'I do,' Rob said quickly. 'Go and change, Sprat, and then we'll all go out to dinner.'

'Oh, Boo, you *are* a bully!'

Rob smiled at Claire when the girl had gone to her room.

'I thought we might eat Italian, at Toni's,' he said.

'Fine. I was going to do raclette but we

can have that another evening.'

'I should have consulted you.'

'Why? Nothing's spoilt. I think I'll change, too.'

The next day they were up and away at six a.m. towards the Oberland. Rob said they must arrive at their destination early or cloud could obscure the views, though he refused to say whither they were bound.

'Got a camera, either of you?' he asked as they climbed into the car.

'I forgot to get a film,' Claire said, regretfully.

'I've got my ciné,' Frances said, patting a black case by her side on the back seat. 'There's a film in needs using up but I've got a spare one. Drive on, James.'

They stopped at eight-thirty for breakfast at a hotel overlooking one of the smaller lakes near Interlaken. Comparatively early as the hour was Switzerland was always busy by eight o'clock each day; many people had already been working for an hour and a half and breakfast was a pause before they continued with it. The good coffee, the bread-rolls and variety of jams tasted good in that setting, where people were already out in small boats and water-skiing. Rob hurried his two companions as they went to tidy up and 'spend pennies' as Frances put it.

'Don't be long,' he called after them.

'Well, old Boo seems to be quite contented,' Frances said, as she combed her long, dark, straight hair in the comparative privacy of the ladies room.

'Oh, good!' Claire decided.

'I don't know about you, though,' the other went on, bowing her lips and outlining them in gloss. 'If you're jumping for joy you don't show it.'

'We can't all be like Angela,' Claire decided levelly.

'I thought her name was taboo?'

'Not to me,' said Claire. 'I never said so.'

'I can't make you out, Claire. I can't really.'

'Why trouble? There may be nothing

about me to make out.'

'Oh, but there is.' Frances said promptly. 'You're deep, Claire. Deep and dark and mysterious, like some of the lakes here. Angela was a village pond, compared. I can see that, now.'

'Shall we go?' Claire waited politely until the other was ready and they then rejoined Rob who was looking impatient.

'Come on, do! As though you weren't beautiful enough already!'

'Oh, thank you,' Frances said lightly. 'I never really thought you cared.'

Mountains began to loom and come nearer, until they shadowed whole valleys and the road was cut through solid rock. In a sort of ampitheatre Rob parked the Jag and then they joined a queue for tickets at a cable-car station.

'I told you we ought to get here early,' Rob said in some irritation. 'Look at this crowd! Cable cars aren't like trains, you know. It could be ages before we get up there.'

Ahead was a large party of holidaymakers,

the men wearing lederhosen and a variety of feathered headgear. One large fat man measured up to Rob.

'You exclusive or summat, lad?' he asked aggressively. 'You want the ruddy place to yersel'? We all got to wait our turn. The good lord didn't make the mountains just for you, tha knows.'

Frances began to giggle and Claire had to smile at Rob's look of utter consternation as he tried to explain that he had not intended to appear offensive and hoped everyone would enjoy their day out. Women were always holding one up, he proceeded, prettying their hair or powdering and puffing.

Frances laughed again and this time the women in the party joined in.

'Ee,' said one, 'that'll be the day when our Jack says I'm prettying an' puffing. I'll be t'last in that queue, I'm telling thee.'

While Rob was still smiling good-naturedly from the encounter the crowd began to surge forward and one of the holidaymakers hooked her arm in his.

'Come on, Luv!' she invited. 'Keep oop wi' me.'

The hair-raising lift, in three stages, by cable-car took them so high their ears popped. They were at the Schilthorn where there was a revolving restaurant with panoramic windows. They were above the snowline and everybody was suddenly reaching for the woollies they had been advised to bring. Rob pointed out the blue-white-purple mass of the Jungfrau, and behind it the Monck, and others leading to the frowning needle-point of the Eiger with its north face black and brooding. There were so many gleaming mountain peaks that Claire felt overwhelmed, and Frances' ciné camera hummed at intervals as they stood on the railed-in viewing terrace with about a score of others. Most people were in the restaurant, seeing the views as incidental bonuses to their drinks and snacks.

'Impressed?' asked Rob, at Claire's shoulder.

'Very. It's marvellous.'

Even as they watched clouds began to drift between the peaks and settle, so that the distant Eiger was soon obliterated and the Monck wore a cloud like a bonnet, down about his ears.

'See what I meant by having to come early?' Rob asked. 'This is what happens.'

Only the Jungfrau shone in the sun, her outline gentle with curves and her eternal snows pristine.

'She's like you,' Rob decided, as Frances' camera whirred.

'Do you mean cold and remote?'

'I rather meant cool and beautiful.'

They looked at each other calculatingly.

'Right!' Frances' voice came incisively. 'I've got a few yards of you two canoodling, now would you mind stepping aside so that I can see the rest of the view?'

ELEVEN

Frances was young and at times inclined to brashness, but she was also very intelligent and Claire had the feeling that she couldn't afford to drop her guard with the girl. When Rob went off to college, and they were left together, Frances decided to try on all her sister-in-law's clothes. Though she was a couple of inches taller they were otherwise of similar build.

'That's fab,' Frances said disarmingly, regarding herself in a satin pyjama suit which Clare hadn't yet worn. Rob had liked it but she wasn't so sure. She felt it was more for the bedroom than for going out to dinner. 'It's very slinky, isn't it? Do you wear it to get Rob going? Does it turn him on?'

Claire said, 'You carry on. I'll make our elevenses.'

Frances appeared in the kitchen wearing her own jeans and a blouse and looking a little sulky.

'What is it about you, Claire, that makes you so aloof? I'm your sister-in-law, you know. You're a member of our family, now. If I'd said a thing like that to old Henry she'd have called me a cheeky young devil, and told me not to ask such embarrassing questions. Mavis would have blushed and been offended, but you don't seem to turn a hair and yet remove yourself to the moon, so to speak, all in an instant, where one can't reach you. Why don't you get mad, or something if I step on your corns?'

'Why should I get mad? You are bright enough to know your questions were in bad taste and so I chose to ignore them. What Henrietta or Mavis do, when you're rude, is their business. I handle such things in my own way.'

'I've been here three days and I'm not much wiser about you and Rob. What's the big mystery?'

'If you think we're going to have a girl to girl chat about your brother and me you're mistaken. When he comes home this evening ask us both when we're together whatever it is you want to know.'

'He's already told me not to be nosey,' Frances said sharply, 'as you no doubt know.' Claire didn't but managed to control her features. 'I think I'll go out and look around the shops. I may get picked up and given lunch if I look lost and helpless enough, so carry on and have your own.'

Claire imagined Frances was trying to shock her, suspecting her of a certain puritanical turn of mind, but as the girl was only a year younger than herself she didn't attempt to be her keeper. In any case Frances was probably much more experienced in the ways of the world than she was. She felt relieved to be alone in the flat, to tidy up and change the flowers and even nip out to the shops. They were dining out with the Herr Direktor and his family, so there was nothing to prepare for evening. When it was time to do her stint at the college, Frances had still not returned, so she had, perforce, to lock her out. When she and Rob returned together there was still no sign, and now Claire really did begin to panic.

'Where can she have gone?' she asked Rob. 'If anything's happened to Frances I shall feel partly to blame.'

'Whatever for?' he asked indulgently. 'Had a row with her, or something?'

'Not really. She asks awkward questions and then accuses me of being aloof when I don't answer. She's determined to get to the bottom of the reasons for our marriage in haste.'

'I know. She had the audacity to ask me if I'd got you pregnant! I soon shut her up. I should imagine she's between boy friends and so has time on her hands for mischief-making. Don't worry for her physical safety. As she had to wait a year to go to Cambridge she spent it doing the overland trip to India on about a hundred pounds. She's done the lot; the Hare Krishna bit, the sari, the namaste, the flower-child. Maybe Ma worried a little but not the rest of us. We'd taught Fanny to be tough and she is. Anyway, here she comes and, apparently, not alone.'

Rob went downstairs to open the outer door. The lift whined back and Frances was laughing, so was Rob and then Claire went into the hall to put a name to the third voice she could hear, which was vaguely familiar. She was surprised to see the tall, brawny figure of Hans-Dieter Müller, the games and gymnastic coach from the college. He was good looking in an Italianate way with dark, wavy hair, sepia eyes and a permanently bronzed skin.

'*Gnadige* Frau,' he bowed formally to Claire though his deep dark eyes had the effect of making a goose walk over her grave momentarily.

'Herr Müller,' she responded. 'Would you like a drink? Do come in.'

'I told you I'd get myself picked up,' Frances was saying brightly. 'I went to look up Rob, at the college, hoping to surprise him, and Hans-Dieter collared me himself. He asked what I wanted with a brother when *he* was free, and he took me out to lunch. Then we watched the boys win at hand-ball, against a Zurich side, and finally those magnificent muscles have been rowing me on the lake. All very nice.'

'Oh, Fraülein,' objected Herr Müller, while obviously enjoying the compliment to his physical prowess.

Claire handed the visitor a Rossi without meeting his eyes. They sometimes regarded her when she was at the college and it was as though they undressed her. It wasn't so much a sinister as a sensual experience.

Rob managed to convey, without appearing rude, that they had to change to take dinner with Professor Gutermann.

'Of course, I understand,' said Hans-Dieter Müller. 'I have so enjoyed meeting your charming sister and – of course – your lovely wife once again.' Claire wished he had transposed the adjectives as she saw Frances positively glare at both herself and him. 'But I, too, have a dinner date. Thanks for the drink. *Gnadige* Frau,' he bowed again, 'Fraülein, Doctor–' Rob saw him downstairs.

'What's this *gnadige* Frau business?' asked Frances.

'They all say that,' Claire quickly explained. 'It means gracious lady. I think it's rather charming.'

'Well, he was a muscle-bound bore if ever I saw one!' Frances suddenly decided.

'But I thought you'd enjoyed your afternoon?'

'*He* did. He's so in love with himself that it becomes painfully obvious after a while. Did I sense an empathy between you and him?'

'Frances! Honestly!'

'Well, he never took his eyes off you. Boo–' she challenged her brother as he returned – 'I believe Hans-Dieter Müller is coveting your wife. I've been telling her so.'

'Well, why not?' Rob asked broad-mindedly, pouring himself another Rossi. 'The time to worry is when she's coveting him. Eh, Claire?' and he contrived to wink at her.

'I suppose stranger things *have* happened,' she tried to say as lightly, but it didn't come out as a joke, somehow. 'He *is* a very physical sort of person and unattached, so I believe. We had better change, I think,' she said as Rob's eyes turned that peculiar navy-blue shade she had witnessed on other occasions. 'We don't want to be late, do we?'

The Gutermanns lived in a handsome house in the college grounds. Frau Gutermann was tiny, dark and extremely friendly. Frances was looking bored until the elder son arrived, a nice looking fellow named Bruno, and that is how he looked, brown-haired, light-brown eyes, wearing the uniform of a lieutenant in the Swiss Army. There were also two young daughters and a boy of eighteen, so quite a crowd sat down to dine eventually.

The meal was delicious, cooked by Frau

Gutermann, herself, and served by a pretty little Italian maid she was training, as any domestic help is difficult to come by in Switzerland, and consisted of slices of salami and sausage, with a green and a potato salad. This was only for starters, however, and then came the main course, which was *cordon bleu,* a dish peculiar to Switzerland, thin veal slices in which was sandwiched a slice of ham and then cheese and the whole fried in butter. Served with rösti, a dish of diced, partly boiled and then fried potatoes, mixed with herbs, it was wholly delicious. They had started the meal with a white wine, but by now they were on to a red, resembling Burgundy and warm and velvety. Frau Gutermann was urging everyone to eat up and have more, but the Swiss habit of having two helpings of the main course was proving too much for Claire and she had to cry enough.

'There is to come a Schwarzwaldetorte,' said Frau Gutermann. 'You must have some. I made it specially.'

'Take a little Kirsch,' said Herr Guter-mann, to Claire, who was on his right. 'It is very good for the digestion.'

'I don't think there is anything wrong with my digestion,' said Claire. 'I simply haven't the capacity. But I will try a little if you say so.'

The clear white spirit was warm and had a wonderful internal effect. When Herr Gutermann asked if she would like more, Claire said yes, and held out her glass.

'I should watch that, Claire,' said Rob from the other end of the table. 'The Professor is trying to make you drunk.'

'Oh, rubbish!' said Claire, deciding she would not be treated like a child. She felt absolutely wonderful, so what was he talking about? She held out her glass a third time.

In the car going home she was very quiet and so was Rob. Frances asked, conversationally, 'Are you going to beat her when you get her back, Boo?'

'Oh, do shut up, Fanny,' Rob said irritably.

'How are you feeling, Claire?' he forced himself to ask.

'Not bad. It was all that creamy cake, you know. I shouldn't have had any.'

Claire had had to go to the bathroom in a great hurry at the end of dinner, where she had proceeded to be very, very sick. She had emerged a pale little ghost with a raging headache and not looked at Rob as Frau Gutermann had said, kindly, 'Maybe the food was too rich for you, Frau Hirst. We are a very gluttonous family.'

'No, no. It was lovely, but I haven't felt very well all day.' It was a white lie and didn't fool either Rob or his sister one bit.

'Would you drink whisky, or gin, after wine?' Rob now asked her. 'Among us we got through quite a few bottles of wine, you know.'

'No, of course not.'

'Well, *Kirsch* is about twice as alcoholic as gin, and so is *Flümli* or *Schwarzke,* so watch your step in future. All are good taken in moderation, but you just drank it, like tea.'

'There's no need to go on!' flared Claire. 'I've got rid of it all, now, and most of my dinner.'

'Oh, don't stop!' Frances begged. 'Other people's rows are so enjoyable. Maybe Claire's an alcoholic and that's the big secret nobody will tell me.'

'Will you be quiet?' Rob asked dangerously, glaring at his sister through the rearview mirror where she grimaced at him cheekily. 'The way you threw yourself at young Bruno, I had no reason to be proud of either of you tonight.'

'Well! Well!' Frances decided, and then collapsed into a huffy silence which she kept up until they reached Bergestrasse, where she went straight off to bed.

Friday was Frances's last day and the couple of days preceding had passed quite pleasantly. She and Claire had gone shopping for presents for the nieces and nephews and lunched out one day, and the younger girl had confided her ambitions both professional and romantic.

'I shan't marry unless I meet an absolutely marvellous man who can sweep me off my feet. Most of my friends are married already to absolute drips. I can't imagine–'

'Perhaps people you consider "drips" have actually swept *them* off their feet?' Claire suggested. 'Look at all the people in our orbit at the moment. I don't see any Miss Worlds or Mr Universes, but I'm sure most of them are happily married or committed in some way.'

Frances looked around and shuddered. 'If love makes most of them lovable, then I've simply never loved,' she sighed. 'I so want to reach peaks, in my career, in my love life–'

'You're like Rob,' Claire teased. 'He's quite a mountaineer, too.'

'And *he* married *you*,' Frances said. 'Was he mountaineering then, Claire?'

'You always have to bring personalities into it,' sighed the other. 'Have you to get anything else?'

'I have to collect the ciné film. It should be ready. Come on!'

The last day Frances was invited to lunch by the college. The two hundred students and male staff gave her a wonderful time, for she was a very attractive girl, and after the meal answered questions about life at Cambridge, for which ten of them were being prepared together with fourteen for Oxford. Later Claire helped her sister-in-law to pack for she and Rob had to leave early for the airport at Zurich next day.

By nine p.m. they had dined and cleared away. Claire had used her raclette set at long last and made a light but interesting and typical Swiss meal. Slices of special raclette cheese were melted on little trays over a methylated spirit burner, and served with buttered boiled potatoes, silverskin onions and gherkins. As the cheese slices were renewed over the burners in the centre of the table, everybody had a wooden 'poker' to prod them until they were soft, bubbly and malleable enough to slide over their potato 'hosts'. It was a novel and quite delightful main course, needing, for the hungry, a substantial dessert, and Claire had made a black-cherry tart which was served with cream. As Swiss milk is about five times creamier than English milk; which is why Swiss chocolate is so famous; so their cream is creamier by far.

'That was really delish, Claire,' Frances had said sincerely as she helped put the dishes away. 'Now let's look at the film I took, shall we? We'll show it on that plain white wall over there as I haven't brought the screen with me. I'm sorry you can't see the new film as it isn't complete. I've quite forgotten what was on the old one, apart from the shots I took at the Schilthorn. But we'll soon see.'

Rob drew the curtains and then settled down in a chair next to Claire and lit up his pipe. He hadn't smoked much since their marriage, indeed he was not a regular smoker. He either had to be *distrait* or completely relaxed to light up a pipe, and Claire hoped he was the latter as she sniffed in the fragrant smoke. She wanted him to be relaxed in her company, at least, if it appeared she had nothing else to offer him.

'Damn!' said Frances, who had just discovered the plug on her projector didn't fit the Swiss socket.

'Fret not,' her brother advised. 'I've got an adapter.'

'Good!' said Frances at length. 'Now, are you all comfy, kiddywiddies? Here we go to the pictures.'

Claire saw a brilliant picture on the white wall of Frances herself, apparently talking to an old man by a river. The old one disappeared and came back with a punt, then the picture clicked off and back on again with Frances, herself, obviously using the camera. This time Rob was seen, with a moustache and the beginnings of a beard, which he stroked lovingly as he obviously posed for his sister, smiling.

'That was last May, remember, when I came to see you in Oxford?' Frances commented.

The film clicked again and then showed

Rob in the punt with a young woman in his arms. They drew apart and Rob frowned at the camera, but Angela laughed and looked very lovely.

'I don't know how long this goes on,' said Frances.

'I do,' and Rob was up like a shot and pulling the plug out of the socket with a flash, 'it stops here and now.' He switched the lights on and faced his sister angrily. 'Are you trying to stir things up between Claire and me deliberately? Do you think she wants to see me cavorting last May like a bull-calf in Spring? She must think that from the first moment of your meeting you became her bitterest enemy. I'm sick of you, Fanny, and in your present rôle you are not welcome here again. Is that clear?'

Claire sat silently clenching and unclenching her hands as she heard the lift whirr downwards and the heavy outer door, below, close with a bang.

'Well,' said Frances, uneasily winding back the film. 'That's what they call a moment of truth, and no mistake. Boo has never spoken to me like that before. I always imagined, out of three brothers, I was his special pet. Now I'm practically told to get lost.'

'He was angry and upset,' Claire told the other. 'He didn't mean that about not being welcome here again. You are, and in any rôle you choose. *I* say so.'

'You're really nice, Claire, and I do mean that. I may have appeared mischievous on and off, this visit, but I swear I didn't know what was on that damned film until I saw it with my own eyes. I didn't want to stir things up between you as Boo says. You *do* believe me?'

'Yes, I believe you, Frances.'

'I think my coming here was a mistake, now. I admit I wanted to satisfy my own curiosity to some extent, but I'm more mystified than ever. You popped up in all our lives like a mushroom, Claire, almost overnight, and yet my brother made you his wife. If I was a novelist I could probably write a book about all the possibilities that situation raises.'

'Sit down a moment, Frances,' Claire said with sudden decision. 'I'm going to tell you the facts of the matter.'

'You needn't,' Frances said, uneasily.

'I know that. But I think you should hear and then all your wilder conjecturings can stop. Also I expect you to keep this fairly confidential. Last Christmas Eve I married Doctor Peter Matthews; I was a hospital sister at the time. The same night he was killed in a car crash after coming off late duty.'

'Oh, Claire! I *am* sorry!'

'I'm over the wallowing. I did it for months and then I crawled back to work, went on a coach-trip holiday where I met Rob, who had just been jilted by Angela. I don't know whether it was a fellow feeling, or that we were two oddments in the party, but we drifted together and almost succeeded in enjoying ourselves on occasion. I had decided to make a new life for myself, certainly by getting a new job, and after Rob and I had exchanged mutual confidences, I jokingly suggested that he ought to marry *me*. He needed to be married to take up this job as the flat – everything had been laid on, and I was a small boat completely adrift at that time. I was more than a little surprised when Rob followed up my outrageous suggestion by inviting me to a Degree Ceremony, in Oxford, to discuss things further. I went because – although I thought we were both being mad – I genuinely liked him. I think the fact that things went ahead proves something.'

'Are you still in love with your Peter?'

'The past is dead. We can't live in the past.'

'I won't ask if you're in love with Rob?'

'No. You may not ask that. I've told you what you wanted to know. The rest is none of your business.'

'Well, thanks for telling me. It won't go any further, I promise you. I think the whole things is awfully romantic. I didn't really believe in romance before. Well, I'll go to bed, now, Claire, after I've packed. Tell Rob I'm sorry when he comes in.'

Claire finally went to bed after midnight, though she knew she wouldn't sleep. She heard the door on the ground-floor open and shut about half an hour later, but the lift didn't whine. Rob was probably, thoughtfully, using the stairs. She held her breath as he entered the bedroom and put his pyjamas on in the dark. He slid quietly into bed cool from the shower and smelling of toothpaste. As usual he turned to face the window, away from her, and not even touching. She knew when he relaxed and slept, because she was still awake, her head thudding with a pain that was more mental than physical and which no pills could ease.

The city was quiet, so it must have been between two and three a.m. when she awoke from an uneasy doze to find Rob reaching out in sleep almost blindly and finding her to draw her to him. She held her breath as she felt the urgency of masculinity in his embrace. She wanted him to wake up, for it to happen naturally and consciously, but instead he pressed sleepy lips to her cheek and murmured, 'Darling! Oh, my darling!'

Why, at that moment, willing as she was to be entranced in his own magical dream, had she to remember that film and the embrace in the boat? Why had she to tell herself it was Angela he was reaching for and Angela whom he was kissing?

A dry sob racked through her being, followed by another.

Rob woke with a start and reached for the bedside light.

'Claire?' he questioned, as the tears rained down her cheeks. 'Claire, what is it?'

She couldn't answer. She felt she wanted to cry a whole lake of tears.

'Has that little brat been upsetting you again?'

'N – no,' she managed to stammer. 'It's not F – Frances. I just wanted to – to cry, suddenly.'

'Then cry, *Liebchen*,' he said, snapping out the light and drawing her roughly to him.

'Cry all you want. I have you safe. They say you have to cry it all out of your system before it gets better.' She didn't know what he was talking about but it was comforting to be held and rocked, to feel one was a child again and that all would be right, again, tomorrow. It was in his arms that she finally fell asleep from exhaustion, and when she awoke and looked up anxiously she was still there, and he was looking at her with tired eyes, as though they had kept vigil while she slept unwinkingly. Passionlessly he stooped to kiss her and asked, 'Better, now?'

'Thank you. Yes. I'm sorry I was silly.'

'Anytime,' he smiled, gently. 'But not too often. You need all that salt. I must grab the bathroom and then get Frances up. We must leave by nine. I couldn't bear for her to miss that damned 'plane.'

'You mustn't be hard on Frances,' she called after him. 'She was very sorry about what happened. I'll get up and take her a cup of tea.'

Frances' leave-taking of her sister-in-law

was somewhat rueful.

'Well, my dear Boo has certainly stopped loving me, and no mistake,' she shrugged philosophically, 'but if it's to start loving you, I'll settle for that and consider I've got a bargain. Goodbye, Claire.'

'Come on!' Rob called sharply. 'Suddenly you have so much to say!'

He was back by lunchtime. Claire had prepared salads – she was learning quickly the Swiss art of making attractive mixtures – there was a green salad, of lettuce hearts, cucumber and cress; a potato salad with a rich dressing of herbs in cream; a celery, walnut and pineapple salad and the wonderful *Schinken,* which is the famous Swiss baked ham.

'My! That looks good!' Rob said, looking at his wife. 'I have decided, *liebe* Claire, that it's time we started living happily ever after.'

'Oh?' she smiled. 'I've mastered the salads, but how do we start doing that?'

'Well, I think we've been too much on the flat, lately. We will lift up our eyes unto the hills. I thought that, tomorrow, we might start with Pilatus. There he is, glowering down at us, so let's go and see what he's really like. Game?'

'I'm game,' Claire agreed.

'It's nice just being on our own again, isn't it?'

'I hope so,' said Claire.

'What do you mean you hope so? We've just got rid of the wicked fairy.'

'You're not to call my sister-in-law names like that.'

He looked at her afresh, and made a playful pass at her chin.

'You're too nice,' he said. 'Everybody tells me what a lucky fellow I am.'

She felt a glow at her heart until later in the day she saw him moving his things back into the room vacated by Frances. When he had finished she went out on to the small balcony and looked at Pilatus, darkening in the twilight.

'Is this the start of being happy ever after?' she asked the mountain silently. 'Just the slogging? No fireworks?'

She sighed as she stepped back into the room, and almost into Rob's arms. A flash of awareness tingled through her being as he held her by the shoulders.

'I thought we might eat Chinese, tonight,' he suggested. 'Any objections?'

'None. I rather like eating by numbers. I'll bet you five francs I manage better with chop-sticks than you do.'

'A gambling woman!' Rob exclaimed. 'I'll take you on. So go and change into your cheongsam, or whatever.'

TWELVE

It seemed to Claire, as the days became weeks, and even months, that 'happy ever after' was a state made up by romantic novelists for their readership's delectation, and that such a thing did not exist in the reality of life. There were little hills of pleasure, certainly, and troughs of disappointment and even, at lowest ebb, almost of despair, but there was chiefly a flat plain of tolerability made up those days and weeks and months which was really the bare bones of living in relative compatability with another person from which the magic elements of being 'in love' were divorced. Thus was Claire towed up the lower slopes of Pilatus, the Klewenalp and Rossberg, the latter providing views of six separate lakes and numerous mountains; privately convinced that subconsciously her husband reached the higher peaks in sublimated alliance with his past love, Angela. She was convinced, now knowing Rob much better, that he would never forgive the girl, but that he would also never forget her. She tried to discover what he really wanted of her, having married her, besides complementing him in his job and having helped to save his face. She had expected they would at least have a physical relationship together, both being young and lusty, and remembered having practically told him so from the very beginning of their mad escapade, though the idea at first had made her extremely nervous. Now the thought that he didn't, perhaps, find her attractive, gnawed at her like a cancer. All her initial inhibitions were overcome every time she saw him afresh each day and her pulses quickened, and each night she felt the same sinking disappointment and disillusion when he knocked a goodnight on her door and walked past, probably to his dreams of past and impassioned love.

Sometimes, when they were together in the flat, she would raise her eyes to find his dark and broodingly upon her. As she questioned with raised brows he would smile, as though to reassure her, and wave his pipe-stem at her and say something like, 'Do you know you wrinkle your nose when you're thinking? You're going to be the only old lady in the world with a smooth brow and a wrinkled nose when you're ninety.'

She fancied he said the first thing which came into his mind at such times, and that he was probably thinking 'Why did I have to marry her?' or something like that.

At other times she would watch him, his hair falling over his brow as he bent correcting a pile of essays, his lashes long and curling over keen, blue eyes. Once she had mentioned these, saying, 'Do you know, you have eyelashes any girl would envy, Rob?' He had pondered, and then said, wryly, 'Don't worry, Claire. I'm one hundred-per-cent boy underneath them!'

But with her he was patient and kind, at times almost tender, as when he had comforted her on that memorable night, but his hundred-per-cent 'boyness' did not demand marital rights of his 'wife', not that he would have to demand, exactly. At the merest beckoning she would have flown to his arms and be hanged for the consequence. When she admitted this to herself she fancied he would think her a forward hussy if only he could read her thoughts.

Autumn brought rain and in early November the first snow fell, wet and miserable.

'We're going shopping,' Rob said one Saturday, 'and we may as well do it in one of the most expensive thoroughfares in the world. Come on!'

They drove to Zurich, with which Claire promptly fell in love, especially the narrow cobbled streets beloved by the antiquarians. She looked in old, bowed windows at dolls' furniture made of silver filigree, and wondered which pampered little darling had received such a gift in bygone days, and what must her dolls' house have been like? She saw the antique clocks, marvelled as Swiss shepherds and their lady-loves came waltzing out, yodelling, as the hour struck midday, and then disbelievingly saw the label which gave the price of such a piece as more than ten thousand pounds.

They lunched at the Goethe-Stübli, where the great writer and philosopher had met with his friends of the day, and Rob interpreted some of the old Gothic scripts on the walls for her benefit.

'He as good as said he would probably make all the same mistakes again a second time round. That erring was learning and the result, wisdom. What do you think, Claire? Would you take a different route through life, if you could come back again?'

'Who knows?' she responded with a question. 'I don't really think so. We act because of what we are, and we would probably be no different born again.'

'Do you think you'd still have married Pete?'

He had mentioned Pete a lot, recently, as though he didn't want her to feel inhibited about her past life.

'Yes. He was part of my emotional life at that time.'

They had calves' liver cooked in a rich sauce and took a warm *rosé* with it, then *kirchetorte* with cream and black coffee.

'Now to business,' Rob said as he helped her into her camel-hair winter coat. 'So far we've just looked. Now we're going to buy.'

She felt one of those rare moments of happiness as he took her gloved hand and towed her down the elegant, wide and expensive *Bahnhofstrasse*, running her past the jewellers' still displaying eighteen-carat gold watches in their windows, and bracelets bright with diamonds, so, he said, she might not be tempted.

'My name's not Rothschild,' he told her.

But they did enter a furrier's. Claire stroked the gloves in moleskin and bear while Rob conversed with an assistant.

'*Meine Frau, bitte?*' the woman indicated that Claire should follow her into a room behind the scenes. Claire looked questioningly at Rob, who shoo'd her off encouragingly. Her camel-hair coat was slid off her shoulders showing the red jersey dress she wore underneath. Next moment she was draped in the elegance of soft grey-white fur. She looked at herself this way and that in the long mirror. She felt rich. She went to show Rob, who promptly laughed, as did the assistant.

'That's wolf-skin,' Rob explained, 'and I was just telling our friend, here, that you look as though Red Riding Hood did get eaten up after all. No that's not you. Try again.'

Claire reappeared in a beaver coat and was again dismissed. Then she looked at herself in the long mirror disbelievingly. She looked wonderful. The coat was black and smooth and beautiful. The assistant nodded full approval, and produced a matching hat, like a bonnet, edged with white miniver, and concealing ear protectors for the bitterness of coming winter. Black gloves with the same edging of miniver completed the picture and she sailed out to confront Rob who took one look and said, 'Right! We'll take that lot.'

'Rob! are you mad? These are sables and cost the earth.'

'So what? Today I own the earth.'

'Rob! be serious. How can we afford these?'

'Because they make you look a million and because my Grandmama left me a few bob more than I thought. Some people are rabbit, other fools may be wolf but you, Claire, are sables. You do me proud.'

Further along the wide street they bought boots, weather-proof and elegant.

'What about you?' she asked.

'I have all the clobber. I've been here in winter before, you know.'

'I don't like you doing all the giving. I haven't given you anything.'

'It's early days,' he told her, meaningfully. 'I'm sure your cornucopaea is well-stocked.'

She reached up and kissed him impulsively on the mouth.

'My goodness, you'll get us arrested!' he said, taking her arm to steer her across the street to the *Parkplatz* where they had left the Jag.

She knew in that moment that she was in love with Rob as deeply as any woman could be. She could not remember how it had been with Pete, only that she had married him knowing there would be a lot of forgiving to do, as she was the strong member of the partnership. But now she was the weak one, the one who loved and was not loved in return, but, rather, tolerated. Rob was the strong one who refused to bastardize his emotions. He may desire her, for all she knew, on occasions, but he would not take from love one part of the whole. He was above his own desires. To him the physical union was only a facet of loving someone. On their wedding day he had teased her, but since then he had scarcely touched her. The agony of loving hopelessly made her want to cry out, sometimes, but she always controlled the impulse.

Then came the crisis in the college which was to have repercussions on their relationship. One student after another wilted and became ill, and soon twelve were confined to bed in the hospital wing. Doctor Oeschker made various tests and announced that they had an outbreak of glandular fever on their hands. Unaffected students laughed and called it the 'kissing disease', but one of the sick boys didn't think it funny.

'Do you know, Sister,' he asked, 'that I have never kissed a girl? I am only interested in my career. It is so damned unfair.'

'I know,' said Claire, comfortingly. 'The virus is very infectious and though it attacks young people, in the main, I've had a sixty-three year old woman laid low with it.'

Some of the patients felt worse in the night and so she arranged to be put up in a room just off the sick-ward. Fortunately the outbreak was confined but she became very tired of answering bells in the night and going to and from the flat by day. She began to look pale and drawn. Rob hauled her aside one day and said, 'I don't want you overdoing things. When are you coming home for a proper night's sleep?'

'I think the worst is over, now. Collect me on Friday evening, if you like. We're sending six boys home to convalesce and the others aren't so bad. They'll probably be back at their studies on Monday, advised to take things easily.'

'Friday, then,' said Rob, and was gone.

On Thursday the snow fell deep and crisp and even and a thrill of excitement ran through the college. Out of doors breath crackled in the crisp air. As Claire prepared to give out the evening medications Hans-Dieter Müller approached.

'Let me push that trolley,' he said. 'You must allow a fellow to help.'

'Thank you, Herr Müller.'

They made the round of the ward giving out placebos, mainly. Doctor Oeschker was a great believer in using psychology to cure. If the sick thought a pill would make them better then a pill they were given, and almost invariably they felt better.

Hans-Dieter helped her wash up in the tiny pantry, later, then said goodnight and left her to go to her room. He turned up the same time the following evening asking if he could help.

'Oh, there's nothing much to do and I'm going home, Herr Müller, when my husband has finished his special coaching class.'

'Then come and have a cup of coffee in my rooms, *gnadige Frau*. See how we bachelors live, eh?'

She went with him out of interest and politeness. There was a spartan sitting-room with sporting prints on the walls, typical, somehow, of Hans Dieter, and a bedroom with bath opening off. He plugged an electric kettle in and ladled coffee into cups.

'Why didn't that lovely snow stay?' she asked from the window. There was grey slush down in the gardens and a drip-drip from the roofs.

'Because Winter, in *di Schweiz*,' he said, 'plays little games with us. It peeps and runs away, like a maiden playing coyly, but then she finds her power and wields it and becomes a tyrant. One day the snow will not go away, little one.'

'I can't stay long,' she said, glancing at her watch as he poured the coffee. 'Only a few minutes.'

'Try that,' he said, looking like Superman with his powerfully developed shoulders. 'It's warming.'

She drank and the coffee was delicious.

'What's in it?' she asked suspiciously. 'It's not Kirsch, is it?'

'No. It's not Kirsch, Schatz. Let me fill you up.'

'It tastes decidedly alcoholic,' she decided, 'but definitely gives one a lift. I feel quite gay.'

'Have more!' he invited, and turned away to fill her cup again with coffee and whatever he fancied improved its taste.

She said, after a third cup, 'I must go,' and tried to stand up but couldn't. Her legs had turned to jelly. She tried again and again failed. Hans-Dieter laughed.

'What did you give me?' she asked, because her mind was amazingly clear and seemed to be floating free of her body.

'Only this. It's very potent.' He waved a bottle at her on which she read the legend Anise, which meant little to her. She thought it was a herb of some kind and remembered her father telling her how he had spent his weekly penny on twenty-four aniseed balls as a child.

Hans-Dieter sat down beside her and put an arm round her shoulders. 'Such a drink makes good girls bad and bad girls very naughty,' he smiled, and then kissed her at great length.

'Look! you lout!' she said angrily, 'I have no intentions of being bad with you. I don't find you in the least attractive. Now help me up and stop being so disgusting.'

He looked hurt, as though it was the first time he had been spoken to like that in his life.

'Oh! Now come on!' he encouraged her. 'You come to my room, what do you think I expect, eh? That you admire this view from the window? All right! all right!' he agreed as she wriggled unavailingly. 'I'll take you to your damned husband. I expect *he's* attractive, eh? I didn't know you were so pure, you English wives.'

'You don't know much,' she lashed him. 'Some of us believe in the common decencies, like people meaning it when they invite one to have coffee.' He hauled her rather roughly to her feet and held her closer than was necessary. 'And yes,' she said ringingly, 'my husband's the most attractive man in the world, if you must know, *and* he's a perfect gentleman at all times.'

The 'perfect' gentleman flung open the

door at that moment and she wondered how much he could have heard. He looked pale and his eyes were very dark and dangerous.

'Take your filthy hands off my wife!' he said grimly.

Hans-Dieter didn't quite know how to assess an English don who had apparently lost his English cool.

'Actually your wife isn't feeling very well, old chap,' he volunteered. 'She can't stand up.'

Rob strode forward and snatched Claire from the other man's grasp, rather as he would have done a rugby ball, and proceeded to prop her up against the outer door. She could scarcely believe her eyes next moment when Hans-Dieter, who was a chunky five-foot eleven, a physical culture enthusiast and no mean athlete, appeared to sail through the air and arrived on his sofa with such force that both he and it were bowled right over. Claire only had time to see his feet peddling madly when she was picked up like a recalcitrant child and carried ignominously down the stairs, across the courtyard and literally thrown into the back of the Jag.

'I feel I ought to explain,' she ventured, as Rob turned on the ignition. 'It wasn't as it–'

'I feel I ought to tell you to keep silence,' Rob said with an almost deadly calm. 'I think it would be wise for you to hold your tongue for the next twenty-four hours. If you don't, you may get the same treatment as that muscle-bound Casanova back there. I'm telling you for your own good.'

'Thank you,' she said, and was silent.

THIRTEEN

Claire didn't sleep much at all that night but had, in the night hours, regained the use of her limbs and developed an inflated sense of outrage. Told to keep silence for twenty-four hours like an insolent child! She would show him. She started over breakfast. She had boiled his two eggs to perfection but was only having a little *Muesli* herself.

'We can't go on like this,' she decided.

Rob turned a page of *Die Zeitung* and didn't respond.

'I'm talking to you,' she rapped her spoon on her bowl and a little milk spilled over on to the cloth. The newspaper, however, didn't falter.

'I went to Herr Müller's room for a cup of coffee, as he had been helping me. I didn't know Anise made you feel like that. I know

I've been foolish, twice, but it won't happen again.'

This time the blue eyes flashed over the paper.

'Is becoming disgustingly inebriated your secret vice, or do you simply do it for my benefit?' The paper was raised again.

'Well,' she quivered, 'if I did it to gain your attention I was obviously wasting my time, wasn't I? Most of the time you scarcely appear to notice me at all. I think you are the most arrogant man I have ever met. Why don't you shout at me or – or hit me, as you threatened? *I* don't care. You may dress me in sables but I'm not a dummy, I'm a woman with feelings and emotions you don't allow me to express.'

'And *he* did?' Rob asked quietly.

She was upon him in an instant, battering at him with her fists, rather as she had done on that occasion in the cottage.

'No he didn't, because I wouldn't let him. But he's not a cold fish. I discovered that.'

Rob held her off, picked up his paper and

disappeared down the stairs. She was so furious and frustrated that she followed him, running down the stairs with tears streaming from her eyes. She tugged at the big outer door to see him opening a gate to the area of garden, opposite, with a private key granted to the tenants of the flats in the street. Seeing her he locked her out, but not to be denied she ran a little way, climbed on a bench and up over the railings. He was sitting with the hated paper held rigidly in front of him, and this she tore away and then breathed hard, waiting to be stricken down with that powerful fist which had sent Hans-Dieter flying.

For what seemed ages their eyes were locked and then, gradually, Rob's twinkled and he began to laugh. She had to join in though the tears were still raining down her face and her legs felt wobbly, not through the effects of alcohol this time but because the intensity of her anger had drained her.

'Oh, Claire!' he cuddled her to him, suddenly. 'Our second row. I can see a year from now, at this rate, we're going to have some dillies.'

'You think we'll still be going a year from now?' she ventured.

'I like to think so. But it will be your decision.'

'My decision,' she sighed. 'Don't you ever make decisions, Rob?'

'I thought I did myself rather well last evening. When a cold fish is prepared to eliminate the hot-blooded opposition, that's quite a decision.'

'Oh, Rob, I didn't mean that about you being a cold fish.'

'Good! By the way, how did you get in here?' he was busily occupied opening the creaking gate.

'I climbed over the railings.'

He looked at the sharp spikes on top and said, 'My God! You might have impaled yourself.'

She took comfort in the knowledge that he sounded as though he would have really cared if she had.

Christmas was approaching rapidly in a white world.

'What do we do about gifts to your family?' Claire asked Rob, raising her eyes from cards she had written to her own friends.

'Absolutely nothing,' he said. 'We stopped all that years ago. Maybe we can Easter at home and then we'll take presents. Have you told your parents-in-law about us, yet?'

'No. I haven't known how to.'

'I can tell you how to, if you're interested. If you've got a card, there, I can add my name after yours and they can conclude what they will. That we're living in sin, or anything.'

Claire looked uncomfortable and Rob shrugged and said, 'It was just an idea. Bad taste on my part. Sorry.'

They went to the Gutermann's for a typical Swiss Christmas lunch of baked hare and a rich sweet made from almonds. On the whole Christmas was a quiet and religious festival, as it should be, but at New Year the whole populace went mad. There were wild parties on New Year's Eve, when Rob and Claire were the guests of fellow teachers Peter and Ida Segal, at a famous restaurant, when everybody uninhibitedly donned fancy hats and false noses and danced and romped into the small hours. Next day bands played in the streets and there was a fancy-dress parade for the children. Rob and Claire had to force themselves to get up and go and see the sights, they were so tired.

'It's early to bed for me, tonight,' Claire yawned, as New Year's Day was drawing to a close and frost rimed the window panes. The next day they were going off with the students and staff remaining in college – some had gone home for the holidays and others preferred catching up on their studies to more physical pursuits – to Alpersdorf, a village not far from Grindelwald, the better-known winter sports ground, where annually the college sports enthusiasts occupied an entire *pension*. Claire was quite thrilled about the idea, and had promised Rob to attend to her instructor and not attempt anything foolish, and she had a bright yellow ski-suit and a blue one and many warm socks and scarves: boots and skis they would hire, Rob promised her.

After ten hours' solid sleep Claire awoke with the sun hurtfully brilliant on the snow. It was obviously going to be a lovely day for the journey. A knock on her door made her heart jump, as Rob had never once intruded since Frances' departure from the flat.

'Come in!' she called, and he entered with a breakfast tray. The coffee was aromatic and there was crisp toast and marmalade.

'My! I *am* honoured,' she said, pushing the hair out of her eyes. 'Is it very late?'

'See for yourself,' he said, thrusting a red box at her, 'and happy birthday!'

She gazed at him uncomprehendingly.

'Of course, the second of January. Oh, Rob! You remembered, and I don't even know when your birthday is.'

'There's time. It's the tenth of May. Well? Open it!'

She opened the box to reveal a thin-banded watch in red gold. The time it told was five past ten but she could scarcely hear any tick.

'Rob, may I, please, kiss you?'

'No, you may not. That is my prerogative.' His lips descended and her heart left her body momentarily. She covered her confusion by saying:

'You're too good to me, Sables, ski-suits, and now this. How can I thank you?'

'Oh, I'm sure you'll find a way. In the meanwhile eat your breakfast.'

It was breathtakingly beautiful in Alpersdorf. The village was picture post-card pretty and mainly unspoilt and at two and a half thousand metres the air was sharp and clean and so clear on days such as this. Once again Claire and Rob shared a twin-bedded room, but she was determined not to be embarrassed by the contact enforced upon them but to act naturally, even to dress and undress in front of Rob as though she did so every day. He, too, appeared to accept the situation as normal and seemed to like to find her available to chat to. He had fixed her up with a middle-aged ski-instructor who had a 'class' of about twenty, including some students from the college, and it was delightful learning something entirely new, and being congratulated on every small advance. Claire was one of the first to learn how to turn on skis, and managed to keep her balance on the first gentle slope they tried, having conquered skiing slowly on the flat. She was also becoming quite a competent German speaker, though she felt she would never learn the Switzer-Deutsch the nationals spoke colloquially, and which Rob had soon mastered. He had told her it was, to the ear, like English when spoken by a Glaswegian, and that if she listened long enough she would pick it up as she was very intelligent.

She had glowed at that, being called 'very

intelligent' by a D. Litt. was no mean compliment.

The first week sped by and Claire's initial aches and pains disappeared as she learnt to enjoy her new prowess. She was a star pupil and she never exceeded doing what she was told. One student, who did, broke a leg like a match stick, and she helped while the local doctor splinted him and he was taken by ambulance helicopter to the nearest hospital. Sometimes she climbed up through the stunted pines to a clearing where she could watch the real skiers come down from the higher slopes on the main run. She had to acknowledge that Hans-Dieter Müller could ski, when she recongized his black and orange ski-suit flash by. He was especially good on the slalom run. But really she went to watch Rob, in a red suit with a flash of white, travelling like the wind, taking the bumps like a bird in flight. She was so proud of his prowess that she ached inside.

On the last day before their return to

Luzern there was to be a competition, with timed runs down the main slope. There were no great prizes, merely magnums of champagne which would then be shared at *aprés-ski* time by all.

The route was lined by spectators, but Claire had found her own private spot. During the night she had been awakened by what she thought was a rumble of thunder, but in the morning it was announced that there had been an avalanche and the slalom run had been closed off. The main competition run was unaffected. She now stood where the two runs divided. There was a red sign closing off the slalom run. It read *HÜTEN SICH! PASSEN AUF!* and *DANGER!* For good measure.

Eighteen competitors swished past Claire, and she knew Rob was last. He had drawn number twenty. Nineteen must be Hans-Dieter Müller, as she hadn't seen him so far. Then she heard the sound of skis on snow travelling at great speed – there was a minute between competitors – and Hans-

Dieter's orange-clad figure came into view. Possibly he recognized her and looked aside; she never knew; but suddenly the red sign and Hans-Dieter were tangled up together and he was in a bank of snow, winded. She rushed to help him up and had just succeeded in getting him out of his skis and upright when Rob came behind them – after one glance at them both, in an apparent embrace – went down the wrong slope from which the sign had been removed.

It seemed to Claire that the whole thing had taken place in slow motion. Rob had shot off into some sort of danger and she had to be with him, find him. She shouted at Hans-Dieter, who was following her, to go back and fetch help.

'You come back, Frau Hirst! I command you!'

She ignored him and scrambled on down the slope, occasionally falling down and rising, whimpering, to rush on. It was a long time before she was confronted by a towering mass of snow which Rob couldn't have avoided had he tried, but where he had gone in and the amount of snow which then had covered him, she couldn't guess at. He was buried well and truly and, regardless of the danger to herself, she began to scrabble in that mountain of snow. It was like trying to find a needle in a haystack, and it was then she heard the dogs and the rescuers coming towards her.

'Come on! Come on!' she urged them, and then fell down in the snow in a dead faint.

'What am I doing here?' she came to, crying, and pushed the brandy flask away from her mouth. 'Are you trying to get me drunk again?' she asked Hans-Dieter. 'How long has it been?'

'Only a few minutes and I am not trying to get you drunk, *gnadige Frau.* I have been told to look after you, keep you out of the way. They know their job, these people. They'll find your husband. I am so extremely sorry I caused this accident. I hope you don't think it was deliberate in any way?'

'Of course not.' She looked miserably at the men poking with steel rods into the snow, and at the dogs, German shepherds, they were, and one was totally white and responded to the name of Gavin. 'What a stupid name for a dog!' she thought. But Gavin was not so stupid as a dog. He whined excitedly and began to dig with enthusiasm. His handler poked gently with his rod.

'Er ist da!' he said triumphantly, and the entire team began shovelling frantically. Rob was brought out stiff, cold and apparently dead.

Claire screamed as he was given artificial respiration.

'Let me! Let me!' she demanded. 'I'm a nurse,' and shoving one rescuer aside she put her lips to Rob's and breathed air into him from her own lungs. She seemed to have the strength of ten women, temporarily, as the adrenalin ran, and only when she was tugged away and told, 'He'll be OK, now,' did reaction set in and great languor overcome her. Hans-Dieter carried her, following the stretcher through the trees, and put her on to the waiting helicopter to go to hospital. As in a dream she saw the white peaks suddenly below and Rob's dear countenance so near and so pale and with an oxygen-mask over his face. She didn't notice his eyes open and observing her as they neared Grindelwald, for her own were raining tears down upon him and she was praying as she had never prayed before.

'I think we can go and see your husband, now,' said the smiling, English-speaking Matron at the select clinic, for Claire was incapable of understanding any German after the night she had just been through, thrust into unconsciousness by a heavy dose of sleeping pills. The previous evening she had been told, 'Now your husband has to sleep and no, you can't see him. He may not go into shock but there's always the possibility and we keep our patients very quiet. Tomorrow is another day and you must get some sleep, too.'

Now the 'tomorrow' which was 'another day' had arrived and she was shown into Rob's private room. He was sitting up in bed looking his normal self and even tossed her one of his normal, assessing glances.

'You look a mess,' he decided. 'Who's the patient, you, or I?'

'Oh, Rob! Don't joke, please. I might have lost you.'

'And would that have been so bad, then?'

'I asked you not to joke, Rob. It would have been hell.'

'Come here, Claire. You're allowed to sit on the bed. I haven't broken my legs. Now what's this about you behaving badly again? I honestly don't know how you can look so demure and be such a little fishwife on occasions. I'm ashamed of you.'

'What are you talking about, Rob?'

'I'm talking about your behaviour yester-day. I've already had one visitor this morning who told me all about it – and you.'

'You mean Hans-Dieter Müller?'

'The same. He explained how he dislodged the danger sign and so was in a clinch with you when I came down, not looking where I was going. He then told me how you dug in the snow and made your hands bleed, and how you berated the rescuers and urged them to go faster, and called the dogs rude names and then shoved the chief of the party out of the way while you gave me the kiss of life yourself.'

Claire looked down at her fingers, covered in sticking plaster. 'Yes, I suppose I was pretty awful and very rude. I have no excuses. It's just that I love you so very much, Rob. I can't help it but I do. I know you don't love me, but I had to let you know why I've behaved oddly from time to time. It wasn't in our contract to fall in love but I'm not apologizing. I hope you'll forgive me for it. I'll try not to be a nuisance as long as you need me.'

The Matron came in and said, brightly, 'I think it's time for our morning nap.'

'You have to be joking!' Rob decided.

'Oh, no, I'm not joking at all, and Herr Doktor Schultz isn't joking, either, when he is making a round and no visitors are allowed. Frau Hirst must go back home, today. Herr Gutermann has called for her, and if you're a good boy we'll send you home tomorrow.'

'Claire!' came after her as she was hustled from the room and down the corridor by a neat little nurse.

'Claire! Save me all over again from this damned woman!'

FOURTEEN

The flat was filled with Spring flowers. Who had been in, Claire didn't know, but blue and white irises shone with daffodils and narcissi from the bowl on the table and the window ledges.

'I'll put bottles in his bed,' Claire decided, and jumped as she almost bumped into Rob in the kitchen. 'What are *you* doing here?' she demanded.

'I live here.'

'I know that. But at the hospital they said tomorrow. You could have a relapse, or something.'

'I don't think so. I'm intending carrying out doctor's orders. After I'd told Herr Doktor Schultz what I thought of him, and that old dragon who runs the place, they were quite precise.'

'I ought to be very angry with you.'

'I know. But you'll forgive me because you love me.'

She looked at him watchfully.

'I haven't put a weapon into your hands, have I, Rob?'

'No. It feels like a key. A key to that happy-ever-after place we've been looking for. You see, Claire, I love you, too. I have done ever since you turned up at the Graduation Ceremony. There seemed to be something of indecent haste about it, and I looked on it rather as the miner regards fool's gold, but it's just become more and more real with time's passing. I was only waiting for you to get over Pete; whom I thought you still mourned when I saw your sad little face on occasion. I couldn't take *his* wife in any way which robbed his memory. I think you have wanted to be generous towards me at times, but I'm not an animal. I can wait. That is, I *could* wait,' he added significantly. 'Suddenly in that hospital, after hearing you speak, I couldn't wait any longer. Wild horses wouldn't have kept me from you.'

He caught her to him and kissed her rapturously so that she seemed to melt into him and they became as one, the same hot blood raging through their veins and the same nerves tingling in a wild harmony.

'How would you like to climb a very special mountain, my love?' he breathed into her hair.

Pilatus was dark against a cold, clear, moon-ridden sky and a star in the east hung like a jewel.

'I should love it,' she said, softly, as he drew her into the bedroom and closed the door to their private heaven against the world.

All the bells in Luzern rang out the midnight hour, and in one bell-tower the little shepherd boy, who seemed eternally to be separated from the little shepherd girl who shadowed him, broke from his moorings and spent the night by accident in her chalet. Between them they stopped the clock, and that's how they came to be discovered next morning.

This Large Print Book for the partially sighted, who cannot read normal print, is published under the auspices of

THE ULVERSCROFT FOUNDATION